THE SORROWS
OF
YOUNG WERTHER

Johann Wolfgang von Goethe

The Sorrows
of
Young Werther

*A new translation, with an Introduction,
by Burton Pike*

THE MODERN LIBRARY

NEW YORK

2005 Modern Library Paperback Edition

Introduction copyright © 2004 by Burton Pike
Translation copyright © 2004 by Random House, Inc.

This work was originally published in hardcover by the
Modern Library, an imprint of The Random House Publishing
Group, a division of Random House, Inc., in 2004.

LIBRARY OF CONGRESS CATALOGING-IN-PUBLICATION DATA
Goethe, Johann Wolfgang von, 1749–1832.
[Werther. English]
The sorrows of young Werther / by Johann Wolfgang von Goethe;
a new translation by Burton Pike.
p.   cm.
ISBN 0-8129-6990-1
I. Pike, Burton. II. Title.
PT2027.W3P55 2004
833'.6—dc22   2003059358

Modern Library website address: www.modernlibrary.com

Printed in the United States of America

INTRODUCTION

Burton Pike

The Sorrows of Young Werther appeared in 1774; it was the first novel of a twenty-five-year-old author. It created a sensation throughout Europe and has retained its extraordinary power for readers in a world far removed from the one in which it was written.

The root of this story's unsettling power is mysterious. Although it follows the decline of Werther and the cycle of seasons over a year and a half, the novel is not straightforward. It lays bare conflicts and questions that can be only pondered, not resolved. It is like a jewel with many facets that refract differently according to how it is held up to the light. The novel is short, but Goethe, turning the facets this way or that, plunges the reader into unfathomable riddles. *Werther* seems to speak directly to something profound in human nature. Critics have offered conflicting interpretations of the novel and of Werther, but something in both novel and character seems beyond explanation.

Werther is a sympathetic, intelligent, sensitive, generous, unpretentious young man governed by his feelings, which he regards as the essence of life. He is an artist but belongs to the upward-striving middle class. His well-connected mother is anxious for him to rise in the diplomatic service, but when he unwillingly tries to subdue his spontaneous feelings and briefly takes a position as secretary to an ambassador, the result is a disaster. Werther's passionate love for Lotte fares no better.

Werther longs to join the infinite through his feelings, to become one with cosmic nature. This is, as he comes to realize, an unattainable goal, a realization mirrored in his passionate love for the unattainable Lotte. He sees but rejects the strictures and confining rules that most people accept in order to live in relative harmony in society. Like his brother-figure Faust, Werther seeks the infinite, but both society and nature set apparently innate boundaries that the individual is not able to transgress. For Goethe these limits seem to be anthropological and biological rather than moral: he treats them simply as the givens of life. (He wrote elsewhere, in one of his maxims, "It has been seen to that trees do not grow up to the sky.") Goethe regards our attempts to outsoar human limits as admirable but potentially destructive. However, outsoaring human limits is precisely the sphere of art, which is capable of weaving together the worlds of everyday life and of exalted feeling. Art—in this case not the sketches produced by Werther, the weak artist, but the novel written by the strong artist, Goethe—transcends the conflict between self and society, self and nature. In this plan Goethe anticipates the philosophy of Schopenhauer and Flaubert's *Madame Bovary*, a nineteenth-century version of *Werther*. (Flaubert was an assiduous reader of Goethe.)

Werther's longing for the infinite, unable to express itself artistically in more than an occasional sketch—he himself often bemoans the limits of his powers of imagination—

threatens to destroy the bonds of society but finally destroys him. The title of his story might better be translated as *The Sufferings of Young Werther:* the German word *Leiden* means both "sorrow" and "suffering."

His passionate longing puts Werther at odds with nature as well as with society as his feelings become increasingly chaotic. He discovers that nature speaks to humankind with a forked tongue. It is tamed and prettified by human beings for their needs and for their notion of what constitutes picturesque beauty, and in this aspect it corresponds to Werther's aesthetic feeling. But as the seasons progress he comes to see nature as violent, ruthless, and raw, an agent of universal destruction.

Never in prose fiction have the paradoxes of living in the world been more searingly posed than in *The Sorrows of Young Werther.* The novel is full of paradoxes. The story is told in letters, an intensely intersubjective form of communication, but it contains only Werther's letters—through which we are told about or can deduce the reactions of others, including the intended recipient of most of them, Werther's commonsense friend, Wilhelm. A sometimes stuffy, sometimes empathetic "editor" (perhaps Wilhelm, perhaps not) is brought in to serve as further contrast to Werther's effusions and to fill in the gaps of his final days. Werther first sees Lotte as a surrogate mother to her crowd of younger brothers and sisters, and he is ecstatic about her pseudomaternal situation; but he has a testy, distant relationship with his own mother, on whom he is financially dependent. He adores Lotte's father and—rhetorically rather than religiously—the Father in heaven, but we hear nothing about his own father. Werther is devoted to the patriarchal idea in religion, but his lodestars Homer and Ossian are pagan. He adores and is insightful about children, and there is something winningly open and childlike in his own nature.

There are also many examples of a strange obliqueness in the novel that deepen its mysterious quality. The reader might make a list of all the families encountered or mentioned in the novel, partial, whole, extended, and metaphorical families: the result is astonishingly complex and strange. To take just one example: Werther, himself close to children, is presented as a quasi-father-figure to Lotte's brothers and sisters. Their real father appears only in a grandfatherly role, and Albert, who becomes Lotte's husband, is never shown in relation to the children. When Werther dies it is the children who clamber over and mourn him, as if *he* were their father.

There are as well many small, oblique details in the novel. Werther says at one point that, suffused as he is with feeling, "I couldn't draw now, not a line, but I have never been a greater painter than in these moments." The reader must ask: how can one be a great artist and not be able to draw a line? Or Werther meets a servant girl at the well who is struggling to put a jug of water on her head to carry it home. He offers to help; she says, "Oh no, sir." But Werther helps her, and she thanks him. Why the contradiction between negation and action? Or Werther says of the housewife he meets with her children that she must be happy in her narrow daily rounds (although of course she isn't, as what Werther tells us about her makes clear) and that she "sees the leaves fall and has no other thought than that winter is coming." What other thought does Werther imagine she should have? How does this thought reflect Werther's own sensibility? Goethe never explains things but presents them in their often baffling ambiguity for the reader to puzzle over.

Werther's excess of feeling is necessarily projected onto others; only in this way does his feeling validate itself. His passionate nature, rejected or criticized by most adults in the novel but beloved of children, awakens something responsive in Lotte. She shows an answering feeling, particularly evident at the dance after the thunderstorm, and later when she is very nearly swept away by Werther's reading of Ossian.

But Werther's exalted feeling is constantly undercut by nature's implacable reality. It meets a stone wall in Albert, whose feelings are pretty firmly under control of his reason. Werther spontaneously kisses Lotte's little brother but notices at the same time that the boy has a runny nose. Little Malchen screams and bursts into tears at the well when Werther suddenly scoops her up in his enthusiasm and kisses her. Werther gets sand in his teeth when he rapturously kisses a note Lotte has written him. His final letter is a rhapsodic flight of metaphor about meeting death, but the nasty consequences of his shooting himself (he does not die for twelve hours) are reported by the "editor" in cold, forensic detail.

And yet Werther is presented sympathetically. The freshness of his senses, his energy, his responses, his generosity, even his exaltation, make the reader see the world in a different light. Goethe seems both to accept and to reject Werther's energy of feeling, as he both accepts and rejects the world of settled order represented by Albert and Lotte. But the wider world of society as presented in the novel is not so settled: it also contains violence and disorder, which Werther understands as a mirror of his inner feelings: the laborer's passion that led him to murder his employer, the wandering madman who has lost his mind (over Lotte, it turns out), the transgression of the brutally chopped-down trees. Werther identifies passionately with all these incidents.

The language of *The Sorrows of Young Werther* deserves special attention. Goethe created in this novel a literary language that overthrows the tradition of decorum, restraint, and neoclassical balance prized by eighteenth-century writers and readers, replacing it with an impulsive language of subjective feeling. His Faust expresses this attitude succinctly: "Feeling is all, / name but sound and smoke / shrouding heaven's fire." Werther's surging feelings can be expressed only by a language of disjunction: of rushing sentences, frequently broken off or run on, of cascades of clauses set off by commas and semicolons, of dashes, exclamations, and exclamation points. Werther sometimes also speaks to himself in the second person. In its language, *Werther* is an early herald of Romanticism, whose "subjective process . . . involves making a world by shattering old forms and inventing new ones more appropriate to what must be expressed. It is the force of urgency motivating the need to express that shatters existing forms," in the words of Fred Nichols. Rendering this urgency has been the guiding principle behind this translation.

Commentators, beginning with Goethe himself, have pointed out that much of this novel is autobiographical. However, it is well to keep in mind what Goethe said about one of his later novels, *Elective Affinities*, "that it did not contain a line that had not been experienced, but no line the *way* it was experienced." In *Werther*, Goethe is very much in control of a novel about a character who spins increasingly out of control. For all the many autobiographical elements and the accounts of his friends and acquaintances that Goethe gathered and wove into the fabric of *Werther*, this novel is carefully organized and composed. The letters are constructed to make the feelings they present come alive. The cycles of seasons in the two parts of the novel are carefully balanced and reflect Werther's changing inner states.

The Sorrows of Young Werther is also a work profoundly interfused with literature: to borrow Kenneth Burke's phrase, it is a book written on top of other books. This helps to generalize and universalize its themes, characters, and events. Homer and Ossian are the major emblematic literary figures for Werther. Homer represents for him the clear patriarchal world that is his model of ideal universal order; Ossian presents dim figures in a murky landscape who are swept away by the language of feeling. Goethe, who did his own translations of Ossian into German, slanted his version in the direction of passionate, sentimental feeling that is more in keeping with Werther's exaltation. The English originals (used in this translation, although the temptation was great to retranslate Goethe's Ossian back into English) are more restrained, more neoclassical, the figures more statuesque. One can see the difference in the preliminary paraphrase of Ossian that Goethe offers in the letter of October 12 in Book Two. *Werther* also contains many biblical tones and overtones, and echoes of *Hamlet* are unmistakable. Then there is Lotte's reading: on the ride to the dance, Lotte is quite firm about rejecting adventure stories and wanting to read only books that reflect her settled environment. But she is overcome by feeling after the thunderstorm, and able to express her emotion only by uttering the name of the poet Klopstock. She nearly succumbs to Werther's passion when he reads Ossian's poems to her, and when he stops, overcome, she begs him to continue.

The character of Lotte is one of Goethe's finest creations. She is a girl of immense charm and empathy who, without losing her fine qualities, rises to assume the burden of becoming a mother to her many brothers and sisters. Endowed with warm human feeling, she has, in contrast to Werther, made rational decisions about her life, but she comes close to being drawn into his maelstrom.

The Sorrows of Young Werther cast a deep shadow forward on European literature. It was instrumental in setting the model of the artist or the artistic temperament that we find in the novels of Balzac and Flaubert, among others, in which a person of superior feeling but weak powers is isolated from an impersonal society. Goethe's novel cast its shadow on Romantic poetry, Schubert's *Schöne Müllerin* and *Winterreise*, the philosophy of Schopenhauer, and Wagner's *Tristan und Isolde*, as well as providing the subject for Massenet's opera *Werther*. When the monster in Mary Shelley's *Frankenstein* undertakes his moral self-education, *The Sorrows of Young Werther* is one of three books (Milton's *Paradise Lost* and Plutarch's *Lives* are the others) that he studies in order to make himself human: "I thought Werter [*sic*] himself a more divine being than I had ever beheld or imagined; his character contained no pretension, but it sunk deep," the monster says.

The fugitive sense we have that our inner feelings are more alive and more genuine than the world outside ourselves, and in conflict with it, is not unknown in our own time. It is often expressed in popular music, literature, television, and movies. The desire both to free the self and to transcend it speaks and sings to us from many sides, including the escape into drugs. We recognize the sorrows of young Werther.

This translation is of Goethe's revised version of 1787, which somewhat toned down and pointed up the first version. (Goethe even included in Werther's letter of August 15 an apology about what an author gains and loses by revising his work!) The edition used for the translation was the Artemis-Gedenkausgabe of Goethe's *Sämtliche Werke,* second edition, edited by Ernst Beutler and others (Zurich, 1961–1966). I am very grateful to Peter Constantine for his constant encouragement and many suggestions, and to Hanne-Lore Boddin and David J. Gordon for their helpful comments.

THE SORROWS
OF
YOUNG WERTHER

THE SORROWS OF YOUNG WERTHER

I have conscientiously gathered everything I have been able to find about the story of poor Werther and here lay it before you, knowing that you will thank me for it. You cannot withhold your admiration and love for his mind and character, nor your tears for his fate.

And you, good soul, that feels the same pressures as he, take comfort from his sufferings and let this little book be your friend, if through fate or your own fault you can find no closer one.

BOOK ONE

BOOK ONE

How glad I am to have come away! Dearest friend, what is the human heart! To leave you to whom I was so attached, from whom I was inseparable, and to be happy! I know you will forgive me. Did not fate seek out my other attachments just to trouble a heart like mine? Poor Leonore! And yet I was innocent. Could I help it that while I found her sister's willful charms pleasantly diverting, a passion was forming in the poor girl's heart? And yet—am I wholly innocent? Didn't I nourish her feelings? Didn't I make fun of those entirely genuine expressions of nature that so often made us laugh, as little to be laughed about as they were? Didn't I— Oh, what is man, that he can grumble about himself! I will, dear friend, I promise you, change for the better, will no longer, as I have always done, chew on the cud of the little bit of unpleasantness that fate puts in our way; I will enjoy the present, and the past will be past for me. Of course you are right, my friend, people would have fewer pains if—God knows why they are made this way—their imaginations were not so busily engaged in recalling past trials rather than bearing an indifferent present.

Be so good as to tell my mother that I'm devoting myself wholeheartedly to her business and will send her news of it very soon. I have spoken to my aunt, and found that she is by no means the evil person we made her out to be at home. She is a cheerful, impetuous woman with an excellent heart. I explained to her my mother's complaints about the part of the inheritance that has been withheld; she explained the reasons, causes, and the conditions under which she would be prepared to release it, and more than we were asking.—In short, I don't want to write about it now; tell my mother that everything will turn out all right. And, dear friend, in this little transaction I have again discovered that misunderstandings and lethargy cause perhaps more confusion in the world than cunning and malice. At least, the last two are certainly more rare.

Otherwise I am quite happy here, the solitude in this paradisiacal region is a precious balm to my heart, and the youthful season in all its fullness warms my often shivering heart. Every tree, every hedge, is a bouquet of blossoms, and one would like to be a mayfly drifting about in the sea of heady aromas, able to find in it all one's nourishment.

The town itself is unpleasant, but round about it an inexpressible natural beauty. This moved the late Count von M ... to lay out his garden on one of the hills that intersect with the most appealing variety and form the loveliest valleys. The garden is simple, and you feel the moment you enter that its plan was not drawn up by some calculating gardener but by a feeling heart that sought its own enjoyment here. I have already wept many a tear for the deceased in the small, dilapidated summerhouse that was his favorite spot and is also mine. Soon I will be master of the garden: the gardener has taken a liking to me even in these few days, and he won't be the worse off for it.

MAY 10

A wonderful cheerfulness has taken possession of my soul, like the sweet spring mornings I delight in with all my heart. I am alone and enjoying my life in this region, which is made for souls like mine. I am so happy, dear friend, so immersed in the feeling of quiet, calm existence, that my art suffers from it. I couldn't draw now, not a line, but I have never been a greater painter than in these moments. When the dear valley mists around me and the high sun rests on the tops of the impenetrable darkness of my woods and only isolated rays steal into the inner sanctum as I lie in the high grass by the falling brook, and closer to the earth a thousand different blades of grass become astonishing to me; when I feel closer to my heart the teeming of the small world among the stems, the innumerable, unfathomable forms of the little worms, the tiny gnats, and feel the hovering presence of the Almighty who created us in His image, the breeze of the All-Loving One who hoveringly bears and preserves us in eternal bliss; my friend, when the world around me grows dim to my eyes, and world and sky rest entirely in my soul like the form of a beloved, then I often yearn and think: Oh, could you express this, could you breathe onto paper what lives in you so fully and warmly that it would become the mirror of your soul, as your soul is the mirror of infinite God!—My friend!—But it is destroying me, I am succumbing to the power of the gloriousness of these apparitions.

MAY 12

I don't know whether deceiving spirits hover over this region or if it is the warm heavenly fantasy in my heart that makes everything around seem like paradise to me. Right outside the village is a well, a well to which I am spellbound like Melusine with her sisters.—You walk down a small hill and find yourself facing a vault from which some twenty steps go down to where the clearest water bubbles forth from marble rocks. The low wall above, which forms the surrounding enclosure, the high trees that shade the place all around, the coolness of the spot, it all has something enticing, something uncanny about it. Not a day passes without my sitting there for an hour. Girls come from the town and fetch water, the most harmless task and the most necessary, which in former times the daughters of kings would perform themselves. When I sit there the patriarchal idea comes so vividly to life around me, how they all, the elders, make acquaintance and court at the well, and how around the well and the springs benevolent spirits hover. Oh, whoever cannot feel that must never have refreshed himself in the well's coolness after a strenuous walk on a summer day.

MAY 13

You ask whether you should send my books.—My friend, I beg you, for God's sake, don't bother me with them! I no longer want to be led on, cheered up, spurred on, my heart surges enough by itself; I need a lullaby, and that I have found in abundance in my Homer. How often do I lull my agitated blood to rest; for you have never seen anything so changeable, so restless as my heart. My friend, do I need to tell you that, you who have so often borne the burden of seeing me swing from grief to excess, and from sweet melancholy to ruinous passion? I treat my little heart like a sick child: whatever it wishes for is granted. Don't spread this about; there are people who would hold it against me.

The ordinary people of the place already know and love me, especially the children. When at the beginning I first went to join them, asking them amiably about this and that, some thought I was trying to make fun of them and told me off quite rudely. I didn't let it bother me, but felt most vividly something I have often noted: people of some standing will always remain at a chilly distance from the common people, as if they thought they would demean themselves by approaching them; and then there are flighty people and nasty jokers who seem to lower themselves in order to flaunt their own high spirits before the poor.

Of course I know that we are not all equal, nor can be; but I am of the opinion that he who thinks it necessary to distance himself from the so-called rabble in order to preserve respect is just as blameworthy as a coward who hides from his enemy because he fears defeat.

Recently I went to the well and found a young servant girl, who had placed her jug on the lowest step and was looking around for some friend to come help her lift it up onto her head. I climbed down and looked at her.—Shall I help you, my girl? I said.—She blushed all red.—Oh no, sir!—she said. With no fuss.—She arranged the ring on her head, and I helped her. She thanked me and climbed up.

I have made all sorts of acquaintances, company I have not found. I don't know what it is about me that attracts people; so many like and attach themselves to me, and it pains me when our paths coincide for only a short stretch. If you ask what people are like here, I have to say: like everywhere! The human race is a monotonous thing. Most people work most of the time in order to live, and the little freedom they have left over frightens them so, that they will do anything to get rid of it. Oh, the regimentation of mankind!

But a quite good sort of people! When I sometimes forget myself, sometimes enjoy with them pleasures that people are still allowed, joking around a table with good company in frankness and good fellowship, taking a long walk, arranging a dance at the proper time, and such things, it has a quite favorable effect on me; but I must avoid thinking that so many other energies that I must carefully conceal still lie within me, all decaying unused. Oh, it so constricts the heart.—And yet, to be misunderstood is the fate of people like us.

Alas, that the friend of my youth is gone! Alas that I ever knew her!—I would say you are a fool, you seek what is not to be found here below; but I had her, I felt that heart, that great soul in whose presence I felt myself to be more than I was because I was everything I could be. Good God! Was there a single power of my soul unused? Could I not unfold before her all the miraculous feeling with which my heart embraces nature? Was not our relation an eternal weaving of the finest feelings, the sharpest sallies, whose variations even to mischievousness were all marked by the stamp of genius? And now!—Alas, the years she was ahead of me led her earlier to the grave. I will never forget her, never forget her steady mind and divine patience.

A few days ago I made the acquaintance of young V ..., a frank youth with a pleasantly formed face. He has just come from academies, doesn't think of himself as wise, but still believes he knows more than other people. He was also studious, as I gather from everything he said; in short, he knows a good deal. When he heard that I sketched a lot and knew Greek (two meteors in this region), he turned to me and displayed quite a bit of knowledge, from Batteaux to Wood, from de Piles to Winckelmann, and assured me that he had read Sulzer's *Theory,* the first part, all the way through, and that he owned a manuscript of Heyne on the study of Greece and Rome. I left it at that.

I made the acquaintance of another good man, the prince's steward, a frank, trusting person. I'm told it's a joy to one's soul to see him among his children, of whom there are nine; people talk especially about his oldest daughter. He has invited me to visit him, and I intend to go as soon as I can. He lives on one of the prince's hunting estates, an hour and a half from here, where he received permission to move after the death of his wife, since living here in town and in the steward's house was too painful for him.

Otherwise, I have run across a few bizarre characters about whom everything is unbearable, the most unbearable their proffering of friendship.

Farewell! You will like this letter, it is completely straightforward.

MAY 22

That man's life is only a dream has occurred to many, and this feeling constantly accompanies me everywhere as well. When I observe the restrictions that lock up a person's active and probing powers, when I see how all activity is directed toward achieving the satisfaction of needs that in turn have no goal but to prolong our miserable existence, and that all reassurance about certain points of inquiry is only a dreaming resignation, since one paints with colorful figures and airy views the walls within which one sits imprisoned—all that, Wilhelm, makes me mute. I withdraw into myself and find a world! Again, more in presentiment and obscure desire than in portrayal and vital power. There everything swims before my senses, and so dreaming I smile on in the world.

All the high-flown schoolteachers and tutors agree that children do not know *why* they want; but that grown-ups too tumble around like children on the face of earth, not knowing where they come from or where they are going, acting as little from true purpose, and just as ruled by biscuits and cakes and birch rods: no one really wants to believe that, but it seems to me something you can grasp with your hands.

I'll gladly confess, for I know what you would say to me about this, that the happiest people are those who like children live for the day, drag their dolls around dressing and undressing them, and cautiously slink around the drawer where Mama has locked up the sweet cakes, and when they finally get their hands on what they want stuff their cheeks with it and shout "More!"—Those are happy creatures. Those too are happy who give showy titles to their rag-and-bone grubbing or even to their passions, and tout them to mankind as stupendous operations for its welfare and salvation.—Happy he who can be like that! But whoever recognizes in his humility where it all ends, whoever sees how nicely every comfortable citizen knows how to trim his little garden into a paradise, and yet sees too how the unfortunate person groans along on his path undaunted under his burden, and all are equally interested in seeing the light of this sun for just one minute longer—yes, he is quiet and forms his world out of himself and is also happy because he is a human being. And then, hemmed in as he is, he still always holds in his heart the sweet feeling of freedom, and that he can quit this prison whenever he likes.

MAY 26

You know my old habit of settling in, putting up some sort of little hut in a pleasant spot and sheltering there in the simplest way. Here too I've found a small spot that attracted me.

About an hour from the town lies a village they call Wahlheim.* Its situation on a hill is quite interesting, and when, taking the footpath up, you come out into the village, you suddenly look out over the whole valley. A good innkeeper, obliging and cheerful in her old age, dispenses wine, beer, coffee; and best of all are two linden trees, covering with their outstretched branches the small square in front of the church that is closed in by peasants' houses, barns, and yards. I could not easily have found so secluded, so inviting a place, and I have my little table brought out from the inn with my chair, drink my coffee there, and read my Homer. The first time, when I arrived by accident under the lindens on a fine afternoon, I found the place so lonely. Everyone was in the fields; there was only a boy of about four sitting on the ground, holding another child about six months old between his feet and against his chest

---

*The reader should not try to locate the places named here; it was deemed necessary to change the real names found in the original. [Goethe's "editor's" note—trans.]

with both arms, so that he served as a kind of armchair, and in spite of the cheerfulness that looked around out of his black eyes, he was sitting very quietly. The sight pleased me: I sat down on a plow that stood opposite and sketched the fraternal pose with great delight. I added the nearest fence, a barn door, and a few broken wagon wheels, everything the way it stood, one thing after another, and found at the end of an hour that I had completed a well-composed, quite interesting sketch without adding anything at all of my own. That strengthened me in my purpose, in future to rely on nature alone. It alone is infinitely rich, and it alone forms the great artist. Much can be said in favor of the rules, about as much as one can say in praise of middle-class society. A person who forms himself according to the rules will never produce anything tasteless or bad, as someone who follows the model of laws and comfort can never become an insufferable neighbor, never a notable troublemaker; but against that, all rules, say what you will, destroy the genuine feeling for nature and its true expression! Say that that is too harsh, rules merely limit, prune only the rank vines, et cetera.—Good friend, shall I give you a simile? It is like love. A young heart is smitten with a girl, spends every hour of his day with her, squanders all his energies and everything he has in order to express every moment that he is totally devoted to her. And then a philistine comes along, a man in some public position, and says to him: My fine young man! To love is human, but you must love in human fashion! Divide your hours, some to work, and dedicate your hours of relaxation to your girl. Calculate your resources, and I won't begrudge you making her a present from whatever remains after your necessities, but not too often, perhaps for her birthday or name day, et cetera.—If the young man does this he will become a useful young person, and I myself will advise any prince to put him in an academy; but his love is over and done with, and if he is an artist, his art as well. O my friends! Why does the stream of genius so rarely burst forth, surging in such great floods and shaking your astounded soul?—Dear friends, on either side of the river dwell the comfortable gentlemen whose garden sheds, tulip beds, and fields of vegetables would be destroyed, people who therefore know how to avert in time with dams and diversions the threatening future disaster.

MAY 27

I have, I see, fallen into rapture, similes, and declamation, which made me forget to tell you the rest of the story with the children. I had been sitting on my plow a good two hours, completely immersed in painterly feeling, which I presented very fragmentarily in my letter to you yesterday. Toward evening a young woman came up to the children, who in the meantime had not moved, carrying a basket on her arm and calling out from afar: Philipps, you are very good.—She greeted me, I thanked her, stood up, stepped closer, and asked whether she was the mother of the children. She said yes, and as she gave the older one a piece of bread she picked up the baby and kissed it with tender motherly love.—I gave the baby to my Philipps to hold, she said, and went into town with my oldest to fetch some white bread and sugar and a small earthenware pot.—I saw all those things in the basket, whose covering had fallen off.—I want to cook a little soup for supper for my Hans (that was the name of the youngest); the biggest brother, the mischief maker, broke my pot yesterday when he and

Philipps were fighting over the porridge scrapings.—I asked about the oldest, and she had hardly said that he was in the meadow chasing around with a couple of geese when he came running up, bringing a hazel switch for his middle brother. I spoke further with the woman and found that she was the daughter of the schoolmaster, and that her husband was off on a trip to Switzerland to retrieve a cousin's inheritance.—They wanted to cheat him of it, she said, and did not answer his letters; so he went himself. If only he has not met with some misfortune, I have heard nothing from him.—It was hard for me to tear myself away from the woman; I gave a coin to each of the children, and gave her one for the youngest as well, to get a piece of bread for his soup when she went into town, and so we parted from one another.

I tell you, dear friend, when my senses are reeling all my tumult is allayed by the sight of such a creature calmly and happily following the narrow circle of her existence, who helps herself through from one day to the next, sees the leaves fall and has no other thought than that winter is coming.

Since that time I am often outdoors. The children are quite used to me, they get sugar when I drink my coffee, and evenings they share my bread and butter and sour milk. Sundays they never miss getting their coin, and if I am not there after the time for prayers the innkeeper has instructions to pay it out.

They are confiding, tell me all sorts of things, and I am especially delighted by their passions and simple outbursts of desire when more children from the village gather.

It has cost me a lot of trouble to relieve my mother's worry: they want to inconvenience the gentleman.

What I said to you recently about painting is certainly also true for literature; all that is necessary is to recognize excellence and dare to speak it, but that is saying a lot in few words. Today I witnessed a scene that, cleanly copied out, would produce the most beautiful idyll in the world; but why "literature," "scene," and "idyll"? If we are to participate in a phenomenon of nature, must one always toil away at it?

If after this beginning you are expecting much that is high and elegant, you will again be sorely disappointed; it's nothing more than a peasant lad who has inspired me to this animated participation in nature.—I will, as usual, relate it badly, and you will as usual, I think, find me exaggerating; it is again Wahlheim, and always Wahlheim, that produces these rarities.

There was a group of people outdoors under the lindens, drinking coffee. Because I didn't quite like them, I remained at a distance under some pretext.

A peasant lad came out of a nearby house and busied himself with fixing something on the plow that I had recently sketched. As his nature pleased me I spoke to him, asked after his circumstances; we were soon acquainted and, as usually happens to me with this sort of people, soon on friendly terms. He told me that he was in the service of a widow and very well treated by her. He spoke so much about her and praised her in such fashion that I soon saw he was devoted to her body and soul. She was no longer young, he said, she had been badly treated by her first husband and didn't want to marry again, and it shone forth so noticeably from his telling how beautiful, how charming she was for him, how very much he desired that she might choose him, in order to extinguish the memory of the errors of her first husband, that I would have to repeat it to you word for word to give you a feeling for this man's pure longing, love, and devotion. Indeed, I would have to possess the gifts of the greatest poet to be able to vividly portray for you at the same time the expressiveness of his gestures, the harmony of his voice, the mysterious fire of his glances. No, no words can express the tenderness that was in his entire being and expression; anything I could recreate would only be awkward and clumsy. I was especially moved by his fearing that I might think suspiciously of his relation to her, and doubt her good behavior. I can only repeat in my inmost soul how charming it was when he spoke of her figure, of her body, which without youthful charms powerfully attracted and bound him. Never in my life have I seen urgent desire and warm longing so pure, indeed I can say, never thought or dreamed it could be this pure. Don't scold me when I tell you that my deepest soul glows when I remember this innocence and truth, that the image of this faithfulness and tenderness pursues me everywhere, and that I, as if inflamed by it myself, thirst and pine.

Now I will try quite soon to see her myself; or rather, now that I think it over, I will avoid doing so. It is better for me to see her through the eyes of her lover; perhaps she would not appear to my own eyes as she now stands before me, and why should I spoil the beautiful picture?

JUNE 16

Why don't I write you?—You ask that and yet you are one of those scholars? You ought to guess that I am fine, that is—in short, I have made an acquaintance that has touched my heart. I have— I don't know.

To tell you in orderly fashion how it happened that I have met one of the most charming creatures will be difficult. I am cheerful and happy, and thus no good at writing chronicles.

An angel!—Ha! That's what everyone says about his, isn't it? And yet I'm not able to tell you how she is perfect, why she is perfect; enough, she has taken my whole mind captive.

So much simplicity with so much understanding, so much goodness with so much firmness, and calmness of soul together with real life and activity.—

What I'm saying about her is all empty twaddle, wretched abstractions that don't convey a trace of her true self. Some other time—no, not some other time, right now, I'll tell you about it. If I don't do it now it will never happen. For, between us, since I began writing I was already three times on the point of laying down my pen, having my horse saddled, and riding out there. And yet I swore this morning not to ride out, but I go to the window every moment to see how high the sun still is.—

I couldn't resist, I had to go out to her. I'm back again, Wilhelm, I'll have my bread and butter for supper and write to you. What bliss it is for my soul to see her in the circle of those dear, cheerful children, her eight brothers and sisters!—

If I go on like this, you'll know as much at the end as at the beginning. So listen, I'll force myself to give you the details.

I wrote you recently how I met the steward, S . . . , and how he asked me to visit him soon in his hermit's lair, or rather his small kingdom. I neglected it, and perhaps would never have got around to it had not chance revealed the treasure that lay hidden in that quiet place.

Our young people had arranged a ball in the country-side, which I found an agreeable prospect. I offered my hand to a good, lovely, but otherwise insignificant girl from here, and it was decided that I would hire a coach and ride out with my dancing partner and her aunt to where the fes-tivity was, stopping on the way to pick up Charlotte S.—You will meet a lovely girl, my partner said, as we drove through the cleared woods to the hunting lodge.—Watch out, her aunt replied, take care that you don't fall in love with her!—How so? I asked.—She is already promised, the aunt answered, to a very fine man, who is off on a trip to arrange his affairs, because his father died and he has to see to a considerable estate.—The news left me rather indif-ferent.

As we rode up to the gate the sun was still a quarter of an hour from the hills. It was quite oppressive, and the women expressed concern about a thunderstorm that seemed to be forming in small, heavy, grayish white clouds around the horizon. I deceived their concern by pretending expertness about the weather, although I too was beginning to fear that our merriment would suffer a blow.

I got out, and a servant girl who came to the gate asked us to walk around a bit, Mamsell Lotte would be right there. I went through the yard toward the agreeable house, and as I went up the steps that led to it and entered the door, my eyes encountered the most charming spectacle I have ever seen. In the hall, six children from eleven to two were swarming around a girl of fine figure, of medium height, wearing a simple white dress with pale red ribbons on arm and breast. She was holding a loaf of black bread and cutting a piece for each of the little ones around her according to their age and appetite, and gave it to each with such amiability, and each one shouted out "thank you!" so spontaneously, after reaching up for so long with its small hands even before the slice had been cut, and now, happy, either scampered off with its slice or, if the child was a quiet sort, went calmly over to the gate to see the strangers and the coach in which their Lotte was to drive off.—I beg your pardon, she said, for making you come in and keeping the ladies waiting. Getting dressed and making all the arrangements for the house while I'm gone, I forgot to give the children their evening bread, and they won't have it sliced by anyone but me.—I paid her an insignificant compliment, my entire soul rested on her form, her tone, her behavior, and I just had time to recover from my astonishment when she ran into a room to fetch her fan and gloves. The little ones were looking at me sideways from some distance off, and I went up to the youngest, a child with the happiest features. He pulled back, just as Lotte came through the door and said: Louis, give your cousin your hand.—That the little boy did, very candidly, and I could not keep myself from kissing him heartily, in spite of his dripping little nose.—Cousin? I said as I held out my hand to her, do you think I am worthy of the happiness of being related to you?—Oh, she said, with an easy smile, we have so many cousins, and I would be sorry if you were the worst among them.—As we left, she told Sophie, after her the oldest sister, a girl of about eleven, to mind the children and greet Papa when he came home from his ride. She told the little ones to do what their sister Sophie said as if it were she herself, which a few expressly promised. But a small, pert, blond girl of about six said: But it's not you, Lotte, we like you better.—The two oldest boys had climbed onto the coach, and on my intervention she allowed them to ride as far as the woods, if they promised not to tease and held on tight.

We had hardly settled down in the coach, the women had hardly got through the proprieties of greeting each other and making observations about their dresses and especially their hats, and the party they were looking forward to, when Lotte had the coach stop to let her brothers off. They wanted to kiss her hand one more time, which the older did with all the tenderness that goes with being fifteen, the other with much fierceness and recklessness. She told them to greet the little ones again, and we drove on.

The aunt asked whether she had finished the book she had lately sent her.—No, Lotte said, I don't like it. You can have it back. The one before was no better.—I was surprised when I asked what sort of books they were and she answered:*—I found so much character in everything she said, with every word I saw new charms, new rays of spirit breaking through the features of her face, features that gradually seemed to unfold in cheerfulness because she felt in me that I understood her.

When I was younger, she said, I loved nothing so much as novels. God knows how happy I was when I could sit down in a corner of a Sunday and with all my heart share in the happiness and misfortune of a Miss Jenny. And I won't deny that these novels still have some charm for me. But since I so rarely get to a book, it has to be one after my taste, and I love that author best in whom I recognize my own world, for whom things happen as they do around me,

*It has been deemed necessary to suppress this place in the letter in order not to give anyone grounds for complaint. Although, basically, no author can really be much interested in the opinion of one girl, and of a young, unsettled person at that. [Goethe's "editor's" note—trans.]

and whose story becomes for me as interesting and after my heart as my own domestic life, which is, of course, no paradise, but on the whole a source of unutterable blessedness.

I made an effort to conceal my emotions at these words. This didn't last long, for when I heard her speak in passing with such truth about *The Vicar of Wakefield,* about*——, I totally lost my composure, told her everything I knew, and noticed only after a while, when Lotte directed the conversation to the others, that they had been sitting the whole time with startled eyes, as if they weren't sitting there. The aunt looked at me more than once, wrinkling her nose mockingly, but that did not bother me in the least.

The conversation turned to the joys of dancing.—If this passion is an error, said Lotte, I will gladly confess that I know nothing better than dancing. And if I have something on my mind and drum out a contredanse on my out-of-tune clavier, then everything is fine again.

How I feasted during the conversation on those black eyes, how those moving lips and fresh, cheerful cheeks absorbed my entire soul! How I, totally immersed in the marvelous content of what she said, often did not hear the words with which she was expressing herself!—You have some idea of this, because you know me. In short, when we stopped in front of the pavilion, I got down from the coach like one dreaming, and was so lost in dreams in the darkening world around that I hardly paid attention to the music echoing down to us from the brightly lit hall.

Two gentlemen, Audran and a certain X—who can re-

*Here the names of several German authors have been omitted. Whoever shares Lotte's applause will certainly feel it in his heart should he read this passage, and no one else needs to know it. [Goethe's "editor's" note—trans.]

member all the names!—who were the aunt's and Lotte's partners, welcomed us at the coach and led off their ladies, and I led mine inside.

We wove around one another in minuets; I asked one woman after another to dance, and it was of course the most unbearable ones who could not bring themselves to offer me their hands at the end and release me. Lotte and her partner began an English dance, and you may feel how happy I was when it was her turn to begin a figure with us! You have to see her dance! She was so wrapped up in it with all her heart and all her soul, her whole body a harmony, so without care, so spontaneous, as if that were really all, as if she were not thinking, feeling, anything else; and in that moment everything else surely vanished for her.

I asked her for the second contredanse; she promised me the third, and with the most charming frankness in the world assured me that she dearly loved to dance the German dance.—It's the custom here, she went on, that every couple that belongs together stay together for the German dance, but my partner waltzes badly and will thank me if I spare him the trouble. Your lady can't waltz either and doesn't like to, but I noticed in the English dance that you waltz well; if you want to be mine for the German dance, go ask my partner, and I'll go to your lady.—I gave her my hand upon it, and we arranged that her partner should meanwhile chat with mine.

Now it began! We were delighted for a while with all the diverse interweaving of arms. How charmingly, how fleetingly she moved! And when we came to waltzing and the couples circled around each other, things got, at the beginning, pretty muddled, because only a few people could do it. We were clever and let them have their fling, and after the clumsiest left the floor, we jumped in and valiantly kept it up with another couple, Audran and his partner. Never have I got started so easily. I was no longer a person. To have the most charming creature in my arms and fly around with her like lightning, so that everything around us vanished, and— Wilhelm, to be honest, I swore an oath to myself that a girl that I loved, and on whom I had a claim, should never waltz with anyone but me, even if it cost me my life! You understand what I mean!

We took several turns around the hall in order to catch our breath. Then she sat down, and the orange drinks I had set aside, which were now the only ones left, had an excellent effect, except that with every canapé that she conferred on a presumptuous neighbor a dagger went through my heart.

In the third English dance we were the second couple. As we were dancing down the row and I, God knows with what bliss, was hanging on her arm and eye, which was full of the truest expression of the purest, most open, enjoyment, we came to a woman I had found odd because of the charming expression on her no longer quite young face. She looked at Lotte with a smile, raised a menacing finger, and with great significance uttered the name Albert twice as she flew by.

Who is Albert? I asked Lotte, if it is not too bold a question.—She was on the point of answering when we had to part to make the great figure eight, and I thought I saw an expression of thoughtfulness on her forehead as we crossed in front of each other.—Why should I keep it from you, she said as she gave me her hand for the promenade. Albert is a fine person to whom I am as good as engaged.—Now that was nothing new to me (for the women had told me on the way), and yet it was entirely new because I had not thought of it in relation to her, she who had in so few moments become so dear to me. Enough, I became confused, forgot myself, and blundered between the wrong couple so that everything got completely mixed up, and it took all Lotte's presence of mind and pushing and pulling to quickly restore order.

The dance had not yet finished when the lightning, which we had already long seen flashing on the horizon, and which I had constantly maintained was a sign of cooling weather, began to become much stronger, and the thunder drowned out the music. Three women left the line, their partners followed; the disorder became general, and the music stopped. It is natural, when a misfortune or something dreadful surprises us in the midst of enjoyment, that it makes a stronger impression on us than otherwise, partly because of the contrast we feel so vividly, partly and even more because our senses have been opened to perception and therefore take in an impression more rapidly. It is to these causes I must ascribe the remarkable grimaces I saw break out on the faces of several ladies. The cleverest one betook herself to a corner, sitting with her back to the window, and stopped her ears. Another knelt down before her and buried her head in the lap of the first. A third pushed between both and embraced her sisters with a thousand tears. Some wanted to go home; others, who knew even less what they were doing, did not have enough presence of mind to control the impertinence of our young poor devils, who seemed to be quite busy snatching away from the lovely lips of the afflicted all the fearful prayers directed at heaven. Several of the men had gone downstairs to smoke a pipe in peace, and the rest of the company did not refuse when the innkeeper's wife hit upon the clever idea of taking us to a room that had shutters and curtains. Hardly had we got there when Lotte busied herself setting up a circle of chairs and, when at her request the company had sat down, gave instructions for a game.

I saw many a person who, hoping for a juicy pledge, pursed his mouth and stretched his limbs.—We'll play Counting, she said. Pay attention! I'll go around the circle from right to left, and you will count as I go around, each one the number that's his, it has to go like brushfire, and whoever stumbles or makes a mistake gets a box on the ear, and so on up to a thousand.—It was fun to watch. She went around the circle with her arm outstretched. "One," the first began, his neighbor, "two," the following one, "three," and so on. Then she began to walk faster, increasingly faster; then someone missed and slap! a box on the ear, and amidst the laughter the following one too, slap! And faster and faster. I myself received two slaps, and with inward pleasure thought I noticed that they were stronger than those meted out to the others. A general laughter and noisy bustle ended the game well before it reached a thousand. The most intimate took one another aside, the thunderstorm had passed, and I followed Lotte into the ballroom. On the way she said: The slaps made them forget the storm and everything!—I was not able to respond.—I was, she went on, one of the most fearful, but by acting energetically to give the others courage I became brave too.—We stepped to the window. There was thunder off to one side, the glorious rain was rustling down on the countryside, and the most refreshingly sweet aroma rose up to us in the fullness of a warm draft of air. She was standing, resting on her elbows, her glance penetrated the scene, she looked up at the sky and at me, I saw her eyes fill with tears, she

placed her hand on mine and said—Klopstock!*—I immediately remembered the magnificent ode that was in her
thoughts, and sank in the stream of feelings she poured
over me with this one word. I couldn't bear it, bent over her
hand and kissed it, covering it with the most blissful tears.
And I looked up at her eyes again— O noble poet! If you
had seen how idolized you were in this glance, after it I
would never wish to hear your so often profaned name
mentioned again.

JUNE 19

I no longer know where I stopped in my story; I know only
that it was two in the morning before I got to bed, and that
if I could have babbled on to you instead of writing, I
would perhaps have kept you up until morning.

I haven't yet told you what happened on our ride home
from the ball, and today I don't have the whole day to do so.

There was the most glorious sunrise. The dripping
woods and the freshened fields all around! Our compan-
ions dozed off. She asked me, didn't I want to join them? I
shouldn't hesitate on her account.—As long as I see your
eyes open, I said, looking at her steadily, there will be no
danger.—And we both stayed awake up to her gate, which
the maid opened softly and assured her in answer to her
question that Father and the little ones were well and all
still sleeping. I left her there with the request to be able to
see her the same day, she granted it, and I came; and since
that time sun, moon, and stars can calmly go about their

---

*An eighteenth-century German poet who gave expression to extreme states
of feeling transcending normal experience.—trans.

business, I know neither day nor night, and the whole world fades away around me.

I am living such happy days, days such as God reserves for His saints; and come what may, I cannot say that I haven't experienced life's joys, its purest joys.——You know my Wahlheim; I am completely settled there, from there it's only half an hour to Lotte, where I feel I am myself and feel all the happiness that is given to man.

Had I thought, when I chose Wahlheim as the goal of my walks, that it lay so close to heaven! How often on my long wanderings have I seen, from the mountain, from the plain across the river, the hunting lodge that now contains all my desires!

Dear Wilhelm, I have thought about all sorts of things, about people's desire to spread themselves out, make new discoveries, roam around; and then again about the inner drive to yield voluntarily to restrictions, to go along on the track of habit without bothering about what's to the right or left.

It is wonderful how everything around attracted me when I came here and looked from the hill into the lovely valley.——There the little wood!——Oh, could you mingle with its shadows!——There the mountaintop!——Oh, could you scan the whole region from up there!——The interweaving hills and familiar valleys!——Oh, could I lose myself in them!—— I hastened there and came back, but without finding what I had hoped for. Oh, distance is like the future! An enormous glimmering oneness lies before our soul, our feeling blurs in it along with our eyes, and we long to let go of our whole being, to let ourselves be filled with all the bliss of a single great, glorious feeling.—But alas! When we hasten there, when there becomes here, everything is as it was, and we stand in our poverty, in our finiteness, our soul thirsting for the refreshment that has slipped away.

Thus the most restless vagabond longs at last for his home country and finds in his hut, on his spouse's breast, in the circle of his children, in the tasks of supporting them the bliss that he sought in the wide world in vain.

When I go out to my Wahlheim mornings with the sunrise and pick my own sugar peas in the garden of the inn, sit down, pull off their strings, and now and then glance into my Homer; when I then choose a pan in the small kitchen, cut some butter, put the pea pods on the fire, cover them, and sit down to watch, shaking them occasionally: then I feel so vividly how Penelope's arrogant suitors slaughtered, carved, and roasted oxen and swine. Nothing fills me so much with a calm, genuine feeling as the traits of patriarchal life, which I, thank God, can weave into the way I live without affectation.

How happy I am that my heart can feel the simple, harmless bliss of the person who brings to his table a cabbage he has grown himself, not just the cabbage alone but all the good days, the beautiful morning he planted it, the lovely evenings he watered it, and as he had his joy in its advancing growth, he enjoys it all again in one moment.

JUNE 29

The day before yesterday the doctor came out from town to the steward and found me on the floor under Lotte's children, some clambering over me, others teasing me, and I tickling them, which occasioned a lot of yelling. The doctor, a very dogmatic marionette, smoothing his cuffs as he talked and pulling out an endless loose thread, found this beneath the dignity of a clever man; I saw that from his nose. But I didn't let it distract me in the least, let him deal with quite rational matters, and went back to rebuilding for the children the houses of cards they had knocked down. The doctor later went around town complaining that the steward's children were already badly behaved enough, Werther was spoiling them completely.

Yes, my dear Wilhelm, children are the closest thing on earth to my heart. When I look at them and see in these small beings the seeds of all the virtues, all the powers that they will one day so urgently need; when I glimpse future steadfastness and firmness of character in their obstinacy, and in their willfulness good humor and ease that will enable them to maneuver through the perils of the world, everything so unspoiled, so of a piece!—Then I repeat over and over the golden words of the teacher of mankind: Unless you become as one of these! And now, my friend, they, who are people like us, whom we should be regarding as our models, we treat as inferiors. They are not supposed to have any will!—Have we then none? And where does the privilege lie?—Because we are older and cleverer!—Dear God, from Your heaven You see old children and young children, and nothing more; and which ones give You more joy Your son proclaimed long ago. But they believe in Him and don't listen to Him—that's old too!—and form their children after themselves and— Farewell, Wilhelm, I don't want to drivel on about it any further.

What Lotte must be to a sick person I can feel in my own poor heart, which is more troubled than many hearts languishing on sickbeds. She will be spending a few days in town with an upstanding woman who according to the doctors is nearing her end and wishes to have Lotte with her in her final moments. Last week I went with Lotte to visit the pastor of St . . . , a small place that lies an hour off in the hills. We arrived around four. Lotte had brought her second sister along. As we entered the yard of the parsonage, shaded by two high walnut trees, the good old man was sitting on a bench before the door, and when he saw Lotte he brightened up, forgot his stick, and ventured to get up to meet her. She ran over to him, made him sit down as she sat down herself, brought many greetings from her father, and hugged his dirty, rebellious, youngest boy, the nattering chick of his old age. You should have seen her, how she busied the old man, how she raised her voice so his half-deaf ears could hear her, how she told him about young, robust people who had died unexpectedly, how excellent the spa at Karlsbad was, how she praised his resolve to go there next summer, how she found that he looked much better, much more cheerful than the last time she had seen him.—In the meantime I was paying my courtesies to the pastor's wife. The old man became quite animated, and since I could not help praising the beautiful walnut trees that shaded us so charmingly, he began, although with some difficulty, to tell us their story.—The old one, he said, we don't know who planted that one: some say this pastor, some say that. But the younger tree back there is as old as my wife, fifty years come October. Her father planted it on the morning of the day she was born toward evening. He was my predecessor in office, and it's impossible to describe how dear this tree was to him; it's certainly no less dear to me. My wife was sitting on a hewn log beneath it the first time I came into the yard here as a poor student, twenty-seven years ago.—Lotte asked after his daughter: it seemed she had gone with Herr Schmidt to the field hands in the meadow, and the old man went on with his story: how his predecessor had taken a liking to him, and the daughter too, and how he had become first his vicar and then his successor. The story had not long been finished when the pastor's daughter came through the garden with the aforementioned Herr Schmidt. She welcomed Lotte heartily, and I must say, I didn't find her bad: a quick, comely brunette, who could well have been entertaining for one's short stay in the country. Her suitor (which is how Herr Schmidt promptly presented himself), a sensitive but quiet person, was reluctant to join our conversation, although Lotte constantly drew him in. What distressed me most was that I seemed to notice in his features that it was more stubbornness and bad humor than limited understanding that prevented him from joining in. This unfortunately became all too clear, as it turned out; for when we were out walking, Friederike with Lotte and sometimes with me, the gentleman's countenance, which was to begin with of a brownish tint, darkened so visibly that it was time for Lotte to pull me by the sleeve and give me to understand that I had been too forward with Friederike. Now nothing vexes me more than when people torment each other, and most of all when young people in the bloom of life, when they could be most open to all its joys, spoil their few good days with sour faces, realizing only too late how irreparable their wastefulness is. This rankled me, and when we returned to the parsonage toward evening and were drinking milk at the table and the conversation turned to the joys and sorrows of the world, I could not help picking up the thread and speaking heatedly against sour spirits.

We human beings complain so often, I began, and it seems to me mostly wrongly, that there are so few good days and so many bad ones. If our hearts were always open to enjoy the goodness that God prepares for us each day, we would have enough strength to bear the bad when it comes.—But our well-being isn't in our power, the pastor's wife replied: how much depends on our body, if one isn't feeling well, nothing feels right anywhere.—I conceded that.—So let us regard it as an illness, I went on, and ask whether there is not a remedy for it.—That sounds reasonable, Lotte said, at least I believe that a great deal depends on ourselves. I know it does with me. If something bothers me and threatens to make me irritated, I jump up and sing a few contredanses up and down the garden, and it promptly goes away.—That's what I meant, I replied: a bad mood is absolutely like sluggishness, for it is a kind of sluggishness. Our nature dwells on it, and yet if we have the energy to pluck up our courage, we work with renewed vigor and find in activity true contentment.—Friederike was paying close attention, but the young man objected that one is not master of oneself, and is least able to control one's feelings.—It's a question here of an unpleasant feeling, I responded, which everyone is glad to be rid of; and no one knows how far his powers go until he has tried them. Certainly, whoever is sick will go to all the doctors, and not refuse the greatest resignation, the bitterest medicines, in order to restore the health he longs for.—I noticed that the honorable old man was straining his ears to take part in our conversation. I raised my voice as I turned toward him: There is so much preaching against vice, I said, I have never heard anyone rail against bad moods from the pulpit. That's the job of the pastors in town, he said, the peasants have no bad humors; yet it would do no harm either, from time to time, it would be a lesson for his wife at least, and for the steward.—The party laughed, and he laughed heartily along with them until he was overcome by a fit of coughing, which interrupted our discourse for a while, after which the young man again spoke up: You call bad humor a vice; that seems to me an exaggeration.— Not in the least, I answered, if that which harms oneself and one's neighbor deserves this name. Is it not enough that we cannot make each other happy, must we also rob each other of the pleasure that every heart can sometimes grant itself? And show me the person in bad spirits who is so good at hiding it, at bearing it alone, without destroying the joy around him! Or are these bad moods not rather an inner annoyance at our own unworthiness, a displeasure with ourselves, which is always bound up with an envy goaded on by foolish vanity? We see happy people whom we don't make happy, and that is unbearable.—Lotte smiled at me when she saw the emotion with which I was speaking, and a tear in Friederike's eye spurred me to go on.—Woe to those, I said, who use the power they have over a heart to rob it of the simple joys that swell up out of that heart. All the gifts, all the obligingness in the world will not for a single moment replace contentment with oneself, which the envious unease of our tyrant has spoiled for us.

My heart was full to overflowing at this moment; the

memory of so many past things surged into my soul, and tears came to my eyes.

Whoever, I exclaimed, says to himself every day: You can do nothing for your friends but leave them their joys and increase their happiness by enjoying it with them. Are you able, if their inner soul is tormented by a consuming passion, shaken by grief, to offer them a drop of relief?

And if the final, most terrifying illness strikes down the creature that you have undermined when she was blooming, and she now lies there in pitiful exhaustion, her unfeeling eye looking toward heaven, mortal sweat breaking out on her pallid forehead, and you stand before her bed like one damned, with the innermost feeling that with all your wealth you are able to do nothing, and fear convulses you inside so that you would give up everything to be able to infuse the dying creature with a drop of strength, a spark of courage.

At these words, the memory of such a scene at which I had been present overcame me with all its force. I put my handkerchief to my eyes and left the company, and only Lotte's voice, calling out to me, "Let us go," brought me to myself. And on the way home how she scolded me for identifying too warmly with everything, it would destroy me! I should spare myself!—Oh, the angel! For your sake I must live!

JULY 6

She is always around her dying friend and is always the same, always the alert, gracious creature who, wherever she looks, eases pain and makes people happy. Yesterday evening she went for a walk with Marianne and little

Malchen; I knew about it and met up with them, and we went on together. Our path led after an hour and a half back toward the town, by the well that is so dear to me and now a thousand times dearer. Lotte sat down on the little wall, we stood before her. I looked around, and oh, the time when my heart had been so alone came to life again before me.—Dear well, I said, since then I have no longer rested in your coolness, have sometimes not even looked at you as I rushed past.—I looked down and saw that Malchen was very earnestly climbing up with a glass of water.—I looked at Lotte and felt everything she meant to me. Meanwhile Malchen came with the glass. Marianne wanted to take it from her. No! the child called out with the sweetest expression, no, Lotte shall drink first!—I was so delighted by the genuineness, the goodness of her exclamation that I was able to express my feeling only by picking up the child from the ground and kissing her vigorously. She immediately began to scream and weep.—You have done wrong, Lotte said.—I was taken aback.—Come, Malchen, she went on, taking her by the hand and leading her down the steps, wash yourself from the bubbling spring, quick, quick, nothing will happen.—As I stood there and saw with what energy the little girl rubbed her cheeks with her wet little hands, with what faith that the miraculous spring would rinse away all the contamination and rid her of the humiliation of getting an ugly beard from the kiss; saw how Lotte said, That's enough, but the child went on rubbing energetically, as if much would do more than a little.— I tell you, Wilhelm, I have never with greater respect attended a baptism—and when Lotte came up I would gladly have thrown myself down before her as before a prophet who has consecrated away a nation's debts.

In the evening, in the joy of my heart, I could not help

relating the episode to a man whose judgment of people I trusted because he has understanding; but what a response I got! He said it had been quite wrong of Lotte; one should never fool children; that sort of thing gives rise to countless errors and superstitions, from which children must be protected early.—Then it occurred to me that this man had had a child baptized eight days ago, so I let it pass and remained in my heart faithful to the truth: we should deal with children as God does with us, who makes us happiest when He lets us stagger on in benevolent delusion.

JULY 8

What a child one is! How one so craves a glance! What a child one is!—We had gone to Wahlheim. The women rode out, and during our walk I believed—in Lotte's black eyes— I'm a fool, forgive me, you should see them, these eyes.—To be brief (for my eyes are falling shut with sleep), the women got in, the young W . . . , Selstadt, and Audran and I were standing around the coach. The women were chatting from the coach with the fellows, who were easy and casual enough.—I sought Lotte's eyes: oh, they went from one to another! But on me! me! me! who was standing there resigned, all alone, they did not fall!—My heart bade her a thousand farewells! But she did not see me! The coach went off, and a tear rose to my eyes. I looked after her and saw Lotte's bonnet leaning out, and she turned to look, alas! toward me?—Dear friend! I hover in this uncertainty, that is my consolation; perhaps she turned around to look for me! Perhaps!—Good night! Oh, what a child I am.

You should see the ridiculous figure I cut when she is spoken of in company! If someone asks me how I like her— Like! How I hate the word! What kind of person must he be who "likes" Lotte, for whom she does not fill every sense, every feeling! "Like"! Recently someone asked me how I like Ossian!

Frau M. is in a very bad way; I pray for her life because I bear with Lotte. I see her occasionally at a friend's, and today she told me of a wonderful incident.—Old Herr M. is a mean, greedy skinflint, who during his wife's life royally tormented and kept a tight rein on her, yet the wife always knew how to make do. A few days ago, when the doctor said she would not live, she summoned her husband (Lotte was in the room) and spoke to him thus: I must confess something to you that could give rise to confusion and vexation after my death. I managed the household as efficiently and cheaply as I could, but you will pardon me for having gone behind your back these thirty years. At the beginning of our marriage you decided on a meager amount for financing the kitchen and other household expenses. As our household grew and our business increased, you were not to be moved to increase my weekly allowance along with our circumstances; in short, you know that in times when things were at their best I still had to make do with seven guldens a week. I took them without arguing and made up the difference every week from the receipts, since no one would suspect the wife of stealing from the cash-box. I didn't waste anything and would have been of easy mind going to meet Eternity even without having confessed it, except that she who will have to manage the household after me wouldn't know what to do, and you could still go on insisting that your first wife needed only that amount.

I spoke with Lotte about the incredible blindness of the human mind, that a person should not suspect something must be going on if someone makes do with seven guldens when he sees expenses of perhaps twice that sum. But I myself have known people who would have taken the prophet's everlasting little jug of oil into their houses without surprise.

JULY 13

No, I am not deceiving myself! I read in her black eyes genuine feeling for me and my destiny. Indeed, I feel, and in this I can trust my heart, that she—Oh, may I, can I express heaven in these words!—that she loves me!

Loves me!—and how worthy I become to myself, how I—I can tell this to you, you understand such things—how I worship myself, since she loves me!

Whether it's presumption, or a feeling of our true relationship—I don't know the person from whom I would fear anything in Lotte's heart. And yet—when she speaks of her fiancé, speaks of him with such warmth, such love—then I am like a man deprived of all his honors and titles and whose sword has been taken away.

JULY 16

Oh, how it runs through all my veins if my fingers inadvertently touch hers, if our feet touch under the table! I pull back as if from fire, but a secret power draws me forward again—all my senses make me giddy.—But her innocence, her uninhibited soul doesn't feel how much these little intimacies torment me. If while we are talking she places her hand on mine, and in conversing moves closer to me, so that the heavenly breath of her mouth can reach my lips— I think I will sink down as if struck by lightning.—And, Wilhelm! If I should ever dare, this heaven, this trust—! You understand me. No, my heart is not so corrupt. Weak! Weak enough!—But is that not corruption?

She is sacred to me. All desire falls silent in her presence. I never know what is happening to me when I am with her; it's as if my nerves are turning my soul inside out.—She has a melody that she plays on the clavier with the power of an angel, so simply and so spiritedly! It is her favorite song, and as soon as she strikes the first note it stills all my pain, confusion, and fancies.

Not a word about the old magic power of music is improbable to me. How the simple song seizes me! And how she knows when to play it, often at a time when I would like to put a bullet through my head! It disperses the darkness and confusion of my soul, and I breathe more freely again.

JULY 18

Wilhelm, what is the world to our heart without love? What a magic lantern is without light! As soon as you put the little lamp inside, the most colorful pictures appear on your white wall! And if it were nothing but that, passing phantoms, it always makes us happy when we stand before them like wide-eyed boys and are delighted by the miraculous apparitions. I could not go to Lotte today, an unavoidable gathering prevented me. What was to be done? I sent my servant there, just to have a person around me who will have been near her today. How impatiently I awaited him, with what joy I saw him again! I would have gladly clasped his head and kissed him if I wouldn't have been ashamed.

We are told about the Bononian stone that, if you place it in the sun, draws the sun's rays and shines for a while at night. That's how it was with the fellow. The feeling that her eyes had rested on his face, his cheeks, on the buttons of his jacket and the collar of his coat, made these things so sacred, so dear! I wouldn't have parted with the lad at that moment for a thousand talers. I felt so happy in his presence.—God forbid this should make you laugh. Wilhelm, are those phantoms, when we are happy?

JULY 19

I shall see her! I exclaim every morning, when I awake and full of cheer look toward the beautiful sun; I shall see her! And I have no other wish for the whole long day. Everything, everything, is devoured by this prospect.

JULY 20

I can't yet agree with your and my mother's idea that I should go with the ambassador to ***. I don't much fancy being a subordinate, and besides we all know that the man is unpleasant. You say that my mother would be happy to see me engaged in some activity: that made me laugh. Am I not active now? And isn't it at bottom all the same whether I count peas or lentils? Everything in the world ends up being a dirty business, and a person who wears himself out for money or honor or whatever else for someone else's sake, without its being his own passion, his own need, is always a fool.

JULY 24

Since it matters so much to you that I not neglect my drawing, I would rather pass over the whole matter than tell you that I have been doing little since.

I have never been happier, never has my feeling for nature, down to the smallest pebble, the little blade of grass, been fuller or more intense, and yet—I don't know how to express myself, my power to represent is so weak, everything swims and totters so before my soul, that I cannot get hold of an outline; but I imagine that if I had clay or wax, I would probably try to form it. If this goes on I will take clay and knead, even if it should be patties!

I began Lotte's portrait three times and prostituted myself three times, which vexes me the more because I used to be very good at likenesses. So I cut out her silhouette instead, and must content myself with that.

JULY 26

Yes, dear Lotte, I will take care of and arrange everything; give me more things to do, often. But there is one thing I would beg of you: not to sprinkle sand on the notes you write me. Today I raised one quickly to my lips and the sand got in my teeth.

JULY 26

I have already sometimes undertaken not to see her so often. But who could possibly hold to that? Every day I succumb to the temptation and make a sacred promise to myself: Tomorrow you'll stay away for once. But when morning comes I again find an irresistible reason, and before I know it I'm with her. Either she said the evening before: You are coming tomorrow, aren't you?—and who could stay away? Or she gives me something to do, and I find it fitting to bring her the answer myself; or the day is simply too beautiful, I go to Wahlheim, and once I'm there it's only a half hour to her!—I am too close to her atmosphere—and zip! I'm there. My grandmother told a fairy tale about a magnetic mountain: the ships that came too close lost all their ironwork, the nails flew to the mountain, and the poor, miserable crew came to grief among the planks crashing together.

JULY 30

Albert has arrived, and I shall leave; even if he were the best, the most noble person, whom I would be ready to subordinate myself to from every point of view, it would be unbearable to see him in front of me in possession of so much perfection.—Possession!—Enough, Wilhelm, the fiancé is here! A good, dear man that one must love. Fortunately, I was not there to meet him! That would have torn my heart to pieces. And he is so honorable, and hasn't kissed Lotte in my presence a single time. May God reward him for it! I must love him for the sake of the respect he has for the girl. He is well-inclined toward me, but I suspect it is Lotte's work more than his own feeling; for women are subtle in these things, and they are right: if two suitors can keep on good terms with one another, however rarely it happens, she will always retain the advantage.

But I cannot deny Albert my respect. His calm exterior is in vivid contrast to the restlessness of my character, which cannot be concealed. He has a great deal of feeling, and knows what he has in Lotte. He appears to be rarely in a bad mood, and you know that is the sin in a person that I hate more than any other.

He takes me for a person of intelligence; and my devotion to Lotte, my keen joy at everything she does, increases his triumph, and he loves her the more for it. Whether he doesn't sometimes torment her with little pangs of jealousy remains to be seen, at least I, in his place, would not be entirely safe from this devil.

Be that as it may! My joy at being with Lotte is gone. Shall I call it foolishness or blindness?—Why does it need a name? Tell it as it is!—Everything I know now I knew before Albert came; I knew that I could make no claim to her, made none, either—that is, as far as it is possible not to desire in the presence of so much charm—yet now the rascal's eyes grow wide when the other actually appears and takes the girl away from him.

I clench my teeth and mock my misery and doubly and triply mock those who would say that I should resign myself because there was no way it could have turned out otherwise.—Get these marionettes off my back!—I rush around in the woods, and when I come to Lotte and Albert is sitting with her in the garden under the arbor and I don't know what to do, I am boisterously foolish and start doing all sorts of clownish things.—For God's sake, Lotte told me today, I beg you, no more scenes like the one yesterday evening! You are frightening when you are so merry.—Between us, I wait for the time when he has something to do; whoosh! I'm out there, and am always happy when I find her alone.

AUGUST 8

Please, dear Wilhelm, I was certainly not talking about you when I scolded as unbearable those people who demand that we resign ourselves to unavoidable fates. I truly did not think that you could be of a similar opinion. But basically you are right. Just one thing, dear friend: In the world an either-or is very seldom met with; feelings and ways of acting are as variously shaded as gradations between a hawk nose and a pug nose.

So you will not take it amiss if I grant your whole argument but yet seek to steal my way between either and or.

Either, you say, you have hopes of Lotte or you have none. Good, in the first case try to carry them through, try to achieve the fulfillment of your desires. In the second case, pull yourself together and try to rid yourself of a wretched feeling that must consume all your energies.—Dear friend! that is well said and—soon said.

But can you ask of the unfortunate person whose life is slowly, inexorably ebbing away in a creeping illness, can you desire of him that he should through a dagger stroke end his misery once and for all? And does not the malady that consumes his strength not also consume at the same time his courage to free himself from it?

Of course you might answer with a related metaphor: Who would not rather let his arm be cut off than risk his life through dally and delay?—I don't know!—but let's not get tangled up in metaphors. Enough— Yes, Wilhelm, sometimes I have a moment of such jumping-up, shaking-off courage, and I would go—if I only knew where.

EVENING

My diary, which I have been neglecting for some time, came into my hands again, and I am astonished how knowingly I have got into this, step by step! How I have always seen my situation so clearly and yet acted like a child, see so clearly even now, without a glimmer of improvement.

AUGUST 10

I could lead the best, the happiest life if I wasn't a fool. It is not easy to find united such beautiful circumstances to delight a person's soul as those in which I find myself now. Alas, it is certain that our heart alone creates its happiness.—To be a member of the charming family, to be loved by the old man like a son, by the children like a father, and by Lotte!—then honorable Albert, who doesn't disturb my happiness by any bad moods, who embraces me with hearty friendship, to whom I am, after Lotte, the dearest thing in the world!—Wilhelm, it is a joy to listen to us when he and I are out walking and chatting with each other about Lotte: Nothing in the world is more ridiculous than this relationship, yet tears often come into my eyes over it.

When he tells me about her upstanding mother, how on her deathbed she gave her house and children over to Lotte and commended her to him, how since that time Lotte has been moved by a quite different spirit, how she, out of care for her management and in her seriousness became a true mother, how not a moment of her time passes without active loving, without work, and yet her cheerfulness and good humor have never left her.—I walk along idly beside him, plucking flowers by the path, carefully gather them into a bouquet and—throw them into the stream flowing past and look after them as they gently swirl downwards.—I don't know whether I have written you that Albert is to stay here and receive from the court, where he is highly regarded, a position with a decent income. I have rarely seen his like for order and industriousness in business matters.

AUGUST 12

Certainly Albert is the best person in the world. I had a remarkable scene with him yesterday. I went to him to take leave, for the desire had come over me to ride into the mountains, from where I am writing you now, and as I was pacing up and down the room my eyes fell on his pistols.—Lend me the pistols, I said, for my trip.—If you like, he said, if you will take the trouble to load them; they are only hanging here pro forma.—I took one down, and he went on: Since my cautiousness played me such a nasty trick I want nothing more to do with them.—I was curious to know the story.—I was, he said, spending a good quarter of a year with a friend in the country, kept a pair of pocket pistols, unloaded, and slept peacefully. Once, on a rainy afternoon, as I was sitting around idly, I don't know where I got the idea that we could be attacked, we might need the pistols and could— You know how it is. I gave them to the servant to polish and load. He was joking around with the maid and, God knows how, the pistol went off with the ramrod still in it, and the rod shot right through the ball of the girl's right hand and smashed her thumb. I had the wailing and on top of that to pay for the treatment, and since that time I leave all arms unloaded. Dear fellow, what is prudence? You can never be quit of danger. To be sure— Now you know that I am fond of people except for their "to be sure"; for isn't it obvious that every generalization suffers exceptions? But man is such a justifier! If he believes he has said to you something overhasty, general, half true, he never ceases to limit, modify, add, and subtract, until nothing remains of the matter. And once started on this, Albert got very deeply into his text. I finally stopped listening to him, succumbed to a whim, and with a lifting gesture pressed the barrel of the pistol to my forehead, above the right eye.—Ugh! Albert said, taking the pistol from me, what are you doing?—It's not loaded, I said.—Even so, what for? he replied impatiently. I can't imagine how a person can be so foolish as to shoot himself; the very thought is repugnant.

That you people, I exclaimed, in order to talk about something have to say right away: That is foolish, that is clever, that is good, that is bad! And what does all that mean? Does it mean that you have got to the bottom of the inner circumstances of an action? Do you know for certain that you can unravel the causes, why it happened, why it had to happen? If you had, you wouldn't be so hasty with your judgments.

You must admit, Albert said, that certain actions are depraved, whatever motives you may give them.

I shrugged my shoulders and conceded the point.—Yet, my dear fellow, I went on, here too you find a few exceptions. It is true that stealing is a vice: but the person who sets out to rob to save his family from imminent starvation, does he deserve pity or punishment? Who raises the first stone against the married man who in righteous anger sacrifices his unfaithful wife and her despicable seducer? Against the girl who in a blissful hour loses herself in the inexorable joys of love? Our laws themselves, these cold-blooded pedants, let themselves be moved and suspend their punishment.

That is quite different, Albert replied, because a person whose passion carries him away loses all his powers of thought and is regarded as drunk, as insane.

O you reasonable people! I cried, smiling. Passion! Drunkenness! Madness! You stand there so calmly, so uninvolved, you moral people! You scold the drinker, loathe the weak-minded, pass by like the priest and thank God like the Pharisees that He has not made you as one of these. I have been drunk more than once, my passions were never far from madness, and I don't regret either: for despite my limitations I have learned to understand how all exceptional people who created something great, something that seemed impossible, have from time immemorial been vilified as drunks and madmen.

But it's unbearable in everyday life too to hear shouted after almost every halfway free, noble, unexpected deed:

the person is drunk, he's an idiot! Shame on you sobersides! Shame on you wise men!

Those are more of your fancies, Albert said. You exaggerate everything and are certainly wrong at least here, in comparing suicide, which is what we are talking about, with great deeds, since one cannot regard it as anything but a weakness. For of course it is easier to die than steadfastly to bear a life of agony.

I was on the point of breaking off; for no argument upsets me so much as when someone comes along with an insignificant commonplace when I am speaking from the fullness of my heart. But I got hold of myself, because I had heard this often, and had more often been upset by it, and I answered him with some heat: You call that weakness? I beg you, don't be misled by appearances. A people that sighs under the unbearable yoke of a tyrant, can you call that weakness if they finally boil over and sunder their chains? A man who, gripped by horror when his house has caught fire, feels all his strength tense and easily carries away burdens that he could barely move when he is calm; someone who, enraged at an insult, goes after six people and overpowers them, are they to be called weak? And, my good fellow, if effort is strength, why should extreme tension be the opposite?—Albert looked at me and said: Don't take it amiss, but the examples you cite don't seem at all relevant.—That may be, I said, I have often been reproached that my art of throwing things together sometimes borders on drivel. Let's see, then, if we can imagine in some other way the state of mind of the person who resolves to cast off the otherwise pleasant burden of life. For only to the extent that we empathize do we have the right to speak about a matter.

Human nature, I went on, has its limits. It can bear joy,

sorrow, pain up to a certain point, but buckles as soon as that point is passed. So the question here is not whether one is weak or strong but whether he can endure the extent of his suffering. It may be moral or physical: and I find it just as strange to say that the person who takes his life is cowardly as it would be out of place to call someone a coward who dies of a malignant fever.

Paradoxical! Very paradoxical! Albert exclaimed.—Not as paradoxical as you think, I replied. You will concede that we call a mortal illness one in which nature is so undermined, partly consuming her powers, partly so disabling them that she cannot restore them, and there is no happy revolution capable of restoring the normal course of life.

Now, my friend, let's apply that to the mind. Look at a person in his finiteness, how impressions work on him, ideas take root in him, until finally a growing passion robs him of all his rational powers of thought and destroys him.

In vain does the calm, rational person observe the miserable man's condition, in vain does he speak to him! Just as a healthy person at a sick man's bedside cannot impart to him any of his strength.

For Albert this was all too general. I reminded him of a girl who had recently been found in the water, dead, and repeated her story to him.—A good young creature who had grown up in the narrow circle of domestic pursuits and worked during the week, and who knew no pleasure beyond strolling around the town on Sunday with friends like herself, wearing a little finery that she had gradually got together, perhaps even dancing at all the big festivals and chatting with a neighbor about some malicious gossip, or the cause of a quarrel, with all the vivaciousness of the liveliest interest.—Her fiery nature finally feels more intense needs, which are increased by the flatteries of men; she gradually loses her taste for her earlier pleasures, until she finally comes across a man to whom an unknown feeling draws her irresistibly, on whom she casts all her hopes, forgets the world around her, hears nothing, sees nothing, feels nothing but him, the only one, longs only for him, the only one. Not spoiled by the empty pleasures of inconstant vanity, her desire draws her straight to the goal, she wishes to become his wife, she wants to find in an eternal bond all the happiness she is lacking, enjoy the union of all the joys she longs for. Repeated promises that seal the certainty of all her hopes, bold caresses that increase her desires, take complete hold of her soul; she hovers in a hazy awareness, is eager to the highest degree in a foretaste of every joy. Finally she stretches out her arms to embrace all her desires—and her beloved deserts her.—Numb, senseless, she stands before an abyss; everything is darkness around her, no prospect, no comfort, nowhere to turn! For he has abandoned her, he in whom alone she had felt all her being. She doesn't see the wide world lying before her, the many others who could replace her loss, she feels alone, abandoned by everyone—and blindly, driven to desperation by the horrible need in her heart, she jumps off in order to suffocate all her torments in an enveloping, embracing death.—Look, Albert, that is the story of so many people! And tell me, isn't that the case with illness? Nature finds no way out of the labyrinth of the confused and contradictory powers, and the person must die.

Woe to him who could look on and say: The fool! If she had waited, if she had let time do its work, her despair would surely have subsided, another man would have turned up to comfort her.—That's just like saying: The fool, dying of fever! If he had waited until his strength returned, his circulation improved, the tumult of his blood calmed down, everything would have turned out well and he would still be alive today!

Albert, to whom the comparison was not yet clear, objected this and that, among other things that I had only been speaking about a naïve girl; but how a person of understanding who was not so limited, who had experience of more relationships, might be excused was something he could not understand.—My friend, I cried, a person is a person, and the little bit of reason that one may have comes barely or not at all into play when passion rages and the limits of mankind press on one. Rather— About that another time, I said, and reached for my hat. Oh, my heart was so full—and we parted without having understood one another. As in this world no one easily understands another.

AUGUST 15

It is surely true that in the world nothing makes a person necessary but love. I feel it in Lotte, that she would lose me reluctantly, and the children have no other notion than that I will always come tomorrow. Today I went out to tune Lotte's clavier, but I couldn't get to it; the little ones were after me for a fairy tale, and Lotte herself said that I should do what they wanted. I sliced their evening bread for them, that they now take from me almost as gladly as from Lotte, and told them the story of the princess waited on by hands. I learn a lot this way, I can assure you, and am astonished at the impression it makes on them. Because I sometimes have to invent some incidental point that I forget the second time, they immediately tell me that it was different the time before, so that now I take care to practice reciting it pat and unchanging in a singing tone. I learned from this how an author, through a second, altered edition of his story, no matter how much better it may have become as literature, must necessarily harm his book. The first impression finds us receptive, and man is so made that he can be persuaded by the most outlandish things; but it strikes root so immediately that woe to him who tries to scratch it out and eradicate it!

AUGUST 18

Must it be, that what makes for man's happiness becomes the source of his misery?

The full, warm feeling of my heart toward living nature, that flowed over me with such bliss, that made the world around me a paradise, has now become an unbearable torturer, a tormenting spirit, that pursues me wherever I turn. When from the rock above the river I used to look across the fertile valley as far as the hills, and saw everything around me sprouting and welling up; when I saw those hills, clad from bottom to top with dense, high trees, those valleys in their many windings shaded by the most charming woods, and the gentle river gliding on among the rustling reeds and reflecting the dear clouds that the soft evening breeze cradled across the sky; when I heard the birds around me animate the forest, and the swarms of millions of gnats danced bravely in the last red rays of the sun, whose last, trembling glance freed the humming chafer from its blade of grass, and the buzzing and weaving around me made me aware of the ground and the moss that wrests its nourishment from my hard rock, and the broom growing down the barren sand hill revealed to me the inner, glowing, holy life of nature: how I gathered it all into my warm heart, felt myself become divine in the flooding fullness, and the glorious forms of the infinite world moved in my soul, giving life to everything. Monstrous mountains surrounded me, abysses lay before me, and torrents rushed downwards, rivers poured beneath me, and forest and mountain resounded; and I saw all the unfathomable forces toiling and creating together in the depths of the earth, and above the earth and under the sky the races of all the kinds of creatures. All, all populated with thousands of different forms, and people nesting and making themselves safe in little houses and ruling in their minds over the wide, wide world! Poor fool! You who consider everything puny because you are so small.—From the inaccessible mountains across the deserts that no foot has trod, to the ends of the unknown oceans blows the spirit of the eternally creative one, rejoicing in every speck of dust that perceives it and lives.—Alas, how often, then, did I long to fly with the pinions of a crane flying above me to the shore of the uncharted ocean, to drink that burgeoning bliss of life from the foaming beaker of the infinite, and to feel for only a moment, within the narrow power of my breast, a drop of the blessedness of that being that brings forth everything in itself and through itself.

Brother, only the memory of those hours makes me happy. Even this effort to recall those inexpressible feelings, to give them voice again, lifts my soul out of itself, and makes me doubly feel the fear of the condition that now envelops me.

Something like a curtain has drawn back from my soul, and the stage of never-ending life transforms itself before my eyes into the abyss of the eternally open grave. Can you say: It exists, since everything passes away? Since everything rolls on by with the passing clouds, so seldom does the whole power of its existence endure, to be torn away, alas, in the stream, pulled under, and smashed against the rocks? There is not a single moment that does not consume you and those around you who are close to you, not a moment in which you are not, must be, a destroyer: the most harmless walk costs a thousand poor worms their lives, a footstep shatters the toilsome edifices of the ants and stamps a small world into a shameful grave. Ha! What moves me are not the great, rare disasters of the world, the floods that wash away your villages, the earthquakes that swallow your cities: what undermines my heart is the consuming power that lies concealed in the universe of nature, the power that has formed nothing that has not destroyed its neighbor, destroyed itself. And so I stagger on in horror. Heaven and earth and their weaving forces about me: I see nothing but an eternally devouring, eternally cud-chewing monster.

AUGUST 21

In vain I stretch my arms out for her in the morning, when I wake groggily from agitated dreams; in vain I seek her at night in my bed, deceived by a happy, innocent dream, as if I were sitting beside her in a meadow holding her hand and covering it with a thousand kisses. Alas, when still half in the toils of sleep I feel cheered and reach out for her—a stream of tears breaks forth from my oppressed heart, and I weep inconsolably toward a dark future.

AUGUST 22

It is a disaster, Wilhelm, my active powers have deteriorated to a restless indifference, I cannot be idle and yet I can't do anything, either. I have no powers of imagination, no feeling for nature, and books nauseate me. When we have lost ourselves, we have lost everything. I swear to you, sometimes I wish I were a day laborer, just to have when I wake up in the morning a prospect of the day to come, an obligation, a hope. I often envy Albert, whom I see buried up to his ears in files, and imagine myself happy in his place! More than once I have awakened with a start, I was on the point of writing you and the Minister to petition for the position at the embassy that, as you assure me, would not be denied. I think so myself. The Minister has liked me for a long time, and has long been after me to devote myself to some kind of business; and for a while I'm really tempted. Afterwards, when I think about it again, and remember the fable about the horse that, impatient with its freedom, lets itself be saddled and bridled and is ridden to ruin, I don't know what I should do—and, dear friend, is not perhaps my longing to change my circumstances an inner, restless impatience that will pursue me wherever I go?

AUGUST 28

It is true, if my illness could be healed these people would do it. Today is my birthday, and early in the morning I received a small package from Albert. When I opened it I immediately saw one of the pale red ribbons that Lotte had on when I met her, and that I had asked her for a number of times since. Along with it were two small volumes in duodecimo, the little Wetstein Homer, an edition I had so often longed for to take on my walks instead of having to drag along Ernesti's. You see! Thus they anticipate my desires, they seek out all the small favors that are worth a thousand times more than those dazzling presents with which the vanity of the giver humiliates us. I kiss this ribbon a thousand times, and with every breath I greedily drink in the memories of the blissful happiness with which those few, happy, irretrievable days brimmed over. Wilhelm, it is the way it is, and I'm not grumbling, life's blossoms are only appearances! How many wither without leaving a trace behind, how few set fruit, and how few of these fruits become ripe! And yet there are enough of them; and yet— O my brother!—can we neglect ripened fruit, despise it, allow it to rot unenjoyed?

Farewell! It is a glorious summer; I often sit in the fruit trees in Lotte's orchard with the fruit picker, the long rod, and pick pears from the top. She stands below and takes them from me when I hand them down to her.

AUGUST 30

Wretched man! Are you not a fool? Are you not deceiving yourself? What is this raging, endless passion? I have no more prayers but to her; no other form but hers appears to my powers of imagination, and I see everything in the world around me only in relation to her. And that gives me so many happy hours—until I have to tear myself away from her again! O Wilhelm! What my heart often urges me to!—When I have sat by her for two, three hours, and have feasted on her form, her behavior, on the heavenly expression of her words, and all my senses gradually become aroused, it grows dark before my eyes, I hardly hear anything, and it seizes me by the throat like a treacherous murderer; then my wildly beating heart seeks to relieve my oppressed mind but only increases its confusion— Wilhelm, I often do not know whether I am still on this earth! And—if melancholy does not sometimes gain the upper hand and Lotte permits me the miserable consolation of weeping out my desolation on her hand—I have to leave, have to go out! and roam around far through the fields, to climb a steep mountain is my joy, hacking a path through a pathless forest, through hedges that scratch me, through thorns that tear me! Then I feel somewhat better! Somewhat! And when sometimes on my way I lie down exhausted from fatigue and thirst, sometimes far into the night, when the high full moon stands above me; when in the lonely woods I sit down on a gnarled tree to give at least the raw soles of my feet some ease, and then doze off in exhausting rest in the dusky light! O Wilhelm! A cell as lonely dwelling, a hair shirt and belt of thorns would be refreshments my soul pines for. Adieu! I see no end to this misery but the grave.

SEPTEMBER 3

I must leave! Thank you, Wilhelm, for having firmed up my vacillating resolution. For two weeks I have been going around with the thought of leaving her. I must go. She is again in town at a friend's. And Albert—and— I must leave!

What a night! Wilhelm! Now I can survive anything. I shall not see her again! Oh, that I can't fly to you, pour out on your shoulder with rapture and a thousand tears, my dear friend, the feelings that storm my heart. I sit here gasping for air, trying to calm myself, waiting for morning, and the horses are ordered for dawn.

Alas, she is sleeping quietly and not thinking that she will never see me again. I have torn myself away, was strong enough in a conversation of two hours not to betray my intention. And God, what a conversation!

Albert had promised me to be in the garden with Lotte right after supper. I was standing on the terrace under the tall chestnut trees and looking toward the sun that was now for the last time setting over the dear valley, the peaceful river. How often had I stood there with her and watched just this glorious play, and now— I paced up and down on the broad walk beneath the trees that was so dear to me; a mysterious tug of sympathy had held me here so often, even before I knew Lotte, and we were happy to discover at the beginning of our acquaintance our mutual liking for this spot, which is truly one of the most romantic that I have seen produced by art.

First you have the distant view between the chestnut trees—oh, I remember, I think I've already written you a lot about it, how high walls of beech trees finally close one in, and a group of shrubs against them makes the avenue increasingly gloomy, until at last everything ends in a small, enclosed place around which all the shudders of solitude hover. I still feel how much at home I felt when I stepped into it for the first time at high noon: I had a faint presentiment of what sort of stage it would become of blessedness and pain.

I had been losing myself for about half an hour in the sweet, languishing thoughts of parting, of meeting again, when I heard them climbing the steps to the terrace. I ran toward them; with a shudder I grasped her hand and kissed it. They had come up just as the moon rose behind a bushy hill; we spoke about this and that and, without noticing, approached the gloomy recess. Lotte went in and sat down, Albert beside her, I also; but my restlessness did not let me sit for long. I stood up, stepped before them, paced back and forth, sat down again; it was a dreadful state. She pointed out to us the lovely effect of the moonlight that at the end of the wall of beeches illuminated the entire terrace before us: a glorious sight, that was so much more striking because we were enclosed in deep shadow. We were silent, and after a while she began: I never go walking in the moonlight, never, without encountering the thought of my departed dear ones, and without the feeling of death, of the future, coming over me. We will be! she continued, in a voice of the most glorious feeling; but Werther, shall we find each other again? Recognize each other again? What do you foresee, what do you say?

Lotte, I said, as I reached out my hand to her and my eyes filled with tears, we will see each other again! Here as well as there meet again!—I could not go on.—Wilhelm, did she have to ask me that, I who had this painful parting in my heart!

And whether the dear departed know about us, she went on, whether they feel when we are happy, that we remember them with warm love? Oh! My mother's form always hovers about me when I am sitting on a quiet evening among her children, among my children, gathered around me as they gathered around her. When I then with a yearning tear look up to heaven and wish that she could look down for a moment at how I am keeping the word I gave her in her hour of death: to be the mother of her children. With what feeling I would cry out: Forgive me, dearest Mother, if I am not to them what you were to them! Alas! I do everything I can; they are clothed, fed, oh, and what is more than anything else, cared for and loved. If you could see our harmony, dear holy one! you would glorify with your warmest thanks the God whom you asked with your last, bitterest tears for the welfare of your children.——

She said that! O Wilhelm, who can repeat what she said! How can the cold, dead letter portray this divine flowering of spirit! Albert gently interrupted her: It affects you too strongly, dear Lotte! I know your soul is very attached to these ideas, but I beg of you—— O Albert, she said, I know you don't forget the evenings we sat together at the little round table when Papa was away and we had sent the little ones to bed. You often had a good book, but so rarely got to read anything.——Was being around that glorious soul not more than everything? That lovely, gentle, cheerful, always active woman! God knows my tears, with which I often in my bed threw myself before Him: for Him to make me like her.

Lotte! I exclaimed, throwing myself before her, taking her hand and wetting it with a thousand tears, Lotte! May God's blessing be upon you, and your mother's spirit!——If you had known her, she said, pressing my hand—she was worthy of being known by you!——Oh, I thought I would perish. Never had a greater, prouder word been pronounced over me—and she went on: And this woman had to leave in the flower of her years, when her youngest son was not six months old! Her illness did not last long; she was quiet, uncomplaining, in pain only for her children, especially the littlest. As the end neared and she said to me: Bring them up to me, I brought them in, the little ones who didn't understand and the oldest who were beside themselves as they stood around the bed, and how she raised her hands and prayed over them and kissed each in turn and sent them away and said to me: Be their mother!—I gave her my hand on it!—You promise much, my daughter, she said, the heart of a mother and a mother's eye. I have often seen by your grateful tears that you feel what that is. May you have for your brothers and sisters and for your father the faith and obedience of a wife. You shall comfort him.—She asked for him, he had gone out to hide from us the unbearable sorrow he felt; the man was torn apart.

Albert, you were in the room. She heard someone walking about and asked who it was and demanded that you come to her, and as she looked at you and at me, with the calm, comforted look that we were happy, would be happy together.—Albert fell on her neck and kissed her and cried: We are! We shall be!—Calm Albert had completely lost his composure, and I was beside myself.

Werther, she went on, and this woman should have left us! God! When I sometimes think how one sees the dearest thing in one's life carried off, and no one feels that as keenly as the children, who complained for a long time that the bogeyman had carried Mama away!

She stood up, I was aroused and shaken, remained sitting, and held her hand.—Let us go, she said, it is time.—She tried to withdraw her hand, but I held it more firmly.—We shall see each other again, I cried, we shall find each other, among all forms we shall recognize each other. I am going, I went on, I am going willingly, and yet if I should say forever I could not endure it. Farewell, Lotte! Farewell, Albert! We shall see each other again!—Tomorrow, I think, she replied jestingly.—I felt that "tomorrow"! O she did not know, when she withdrew her hand from mine— They went down the avenue of trees, I stood up, looked after them in the moonlight and threw myself on the ground and wept bitterly and jumped up and ran out onto the terrace and saw there down below in the shadow of the high linden trees her white dress shimmering toward the garden gate; I stretched out my arms, and it disappeared.

BOOK TWO

BOOK TWO

We arrived here yesterday. The ambassador is unwell, and so will stop here for a few days. If only he were not so disagreeable, all would be well. I see, I see, fate has reserved hard trials for me! But have courage! An easy mind bears everything! An easy mind? That makes me laugh even as the words flow from my pen. Oh, a little lighter blood would make me the happiest person under the sun. What! Where others with their bit of energy and talent strut around in smug self-satisfaction, I despair of my energy, my gifts? Dear God, who gave them to me, why did You not keep back half and give me self-confidence and modest contentment!

Patience! Patience! It will get better. For I tell you, dear friend, you are right. Since I am thrown in among the common people every day and see what they are doing and how they manage, I feel much better about myself. Of course, since we are so made that we compare everything with ourselves and ourselves with everything, happiness or misery lies in the objects we associate ourselves with, and in this there is nothing more dangerous than solitude. The power of our imagination, driven by nature to elevate itself, nourished by the fantastic images of literature, raises up a series of beings of whom we are the lowest, and everything outside ourselves seems more glorious, every other person more perfect. And that happens quite naturally. We feel so often that we are lacking so much, and just what we lack another person often seems to possess, to which we also add everything that *we* possess, and project a certain ideal contentment on top of it. And thus the other person is made happy, complete, and perfect, a creature of our own making.

On the other hand, if with all our weakness and laboriousness we just keep on working, we often find that for all our aimlessness and random maneuvering we get further than others with their sails and rudders—and—it's a true feeling of oneself when one keeps up with others or even gets ahead of them.

NOVEMBER 26, 1771

I am beginning to find it, to some extent, quite tolerable here. The best is that there is enough to do; and then the many different kinds of people, all sorts of new figures, make a colorful spectacle for my soul. I have made the acquaintance of Count C . . . , a man I have come to respect more every day, an expansive, open mind, who is not cold because he has many responsibilities, and from whose company so much feeling for friendship and love shines forth. He took an interest in me when I had some business to conduct with him, and he noticed from my first words that we understood each other, that he could talk with me as with few others. And I cannot praise his open behavior toward me highly enough. There is no such genuine, warm joy in the world as seeing a great soul that opens itself up to one.

DECEMBER 24, 1771

The ambassador vexes me greatly, I saw it coming. He is the most punctilious idiot imaginable; puts one foot in front of the other and is as long-winded as an old aunt; a person who is never satisfied with himself, and who consequently can never be satisfied with what anyone else does. I like to work quickly, the way it stands is the way it stays: but he is capable of giving a document back to me and saying: It's good, but look through it, one can always find a better word, a more appropriate preposition. It drives me mad. No *and*, no conjunction can be omitted, and he is a bitter enemy of all the inversions of word order that sometime slip through my pen; if one does not plane down his sentences according to the traditional rhythm, he doesn't understand a word of them. It's torture having to deal with such a person.

Count C . . . 's confidence is the only thing that works to my advantage. He told me quite openly recently how dissatisfied he is with the slowness and pettiness of my ambassador. People make things difficult for themselves and others; still, he said, one had to resign oneself to it, like a traveler who has to get over a mountain. Of course if the mountain were not there the path would be much shorter and easier, but it is there, and one has to climb over it!—

My superior also feels that the Count prefers me to him, and that annoys him; he seizes every opportunity to denigrate the Count to me. I answer him back, as is only natural, and that makes matters worse. Yesterday he infuriated me, for he meant me too: the Count was fairly good in worldly affairs, he has great ease in working and writes a good hand; but like all belletrists he lacks thorough erudition. He made a face as if to say: Do you feel the sting? But it did not affect me, I despised the person who could think and behave in such a fashion. I stood up to him with some vehemence. I said the Count was a man who deserved respect for his character as well as his knowledge. I have, I said, never known anyone who had so successfully opened his mind so broadly to innumerable things and yet maintained this activity in his daily life.—This fell on deaf ears, and I took my leave so as not to swallow more gall in further argument.

And it is all your fault, all you who have nattered me into the yoke and preached to me so much about being active. Being active! If he who plants potatoes and rides to town to sell his grain is not doing more than I, I will spend the next ten years wearing myself out in the galleys to which I am now chained.

And the splendid misery, the boredom among these nasty people, that one sees here side by side! Their social jealousy, how intently they watch and wait just to win a tiny advantage over one another; the most wretched, most miserable passions, with no attempt at concealment. There is a woman, for example, who goes around telling everyone about her noble rank and her country, so that every stranger must think she is a fool, building castles in the air about her bit of nobility and her country's reputation.—But it is much worse: this woman is actually from these parts, daughter of a government clerk.—I cannot understand humankind that has so little sense as to prostitute itself so crudely.

Of course I notice more every day, my friend, how foolish it is to judge others by oneself. And because I am so preoccupied with myself and this heart is so tempestuous— Oh, I gladly let the others go their way, if only they would let me go mine.

The disastrous middle-class relationships are what irritate me most. Of course I know as well as anyone how necessary the distinction among classes is, how many advantages I myself derive from it: but it shouldn't stand in my way just where I could enjoy a little pleasure, a shimmer of happiness on this earth. On a walk lately I met a Fräulein B . . . , a charming creature who has managed to keep a great deal of spontaneity in her formal aristocratic life. In talking we took a liking to each other, and as we parted I asked permission to call on her. She granted it with such candidness that I could hardly await the appropriate moment to go there. She is not from here, and lives in the house of an aunt. I didn't like the old woman's face: I paid her a great deal of attention, directed my conversation mostly to her, but in less than half an hour I had pretty well understood what the girl confessed to me afterwards: that in her old age her dear aunt lacked everything, spirit, a decent property, and had no other support than the rank of her ancestors, no protection but the class within which she barricaded herself, and no enjoyment but looking down from her high story on middle-class heads. She was said to have been beautiful in her youth and to have frittered her life away, first tormenting many a young man with her selfishness, and in her more mature years cowering in obedience to an old officer, who for this price and a modest dowry spent the bronze years with her and died. Now in her iron age she finds herself alone, and no one would pay any attention to her if her niece were not so charming.

JANUARY 8, 1772

What kind of people are those whose whole soul is based on ceremony, all of whose thoughts and endeavors are for years directed at how they can move up one chair at the table! And it's not that they would otherwise not have things to do: no, rather tasks pile up just because the important matters are stalled by small vexations over advancement. Last week there was some bickering on the sleigh ride, and the whole fun was spoiled.

The fools who don't see that it really never depends on one's place, and that he who has first place so seldom plays the first role! How many kings are ruled by their ministers, how many ministers by their secretaries! And who then is the first? The person, I think, who understands where the others are and has so much power or cunning that he can harness their energies and passions to the execution of his plans.

JANUARY 20

I must write you, dear Lotte, here in the taproom of a humble peasant inn in which I have taken refuge from a severe storm. As long as I have been going around among the alien, to my heart totally alien, people of the sad nest D..., I have not had a moment, not one, in which my heart would have bade me to write you; but now, in this humble place, in this solitude, in this confinement, as snow and hail rage against my windowpane, here you were my first thought. As I came in I was overcome by your form, by the memory of you, O Lotte! So sacred, so warm! Good God! My first happy moment again.

If you could see me, dearest friend, in the flood of distractions! How dried up my senses become; not a single instant when my heart is full, not an hour that is blessed! Nothing! Nothing! It's as if I'm standing in front of a cabinet of curiosities and see the little men and little horses move around before me, and often I ask myself whether it is not an optical illusion. I play along with it, or rather I am played like a marionette, and sometimes grasp my neighbor by his wooden hand and pull back, horrified. Evenings I plan to enjoy the sunrise, and don't get out of bed; during the day I look forward to enjoying the moonlight, and remain in my room. I really don't know why I get up, why I go to bed.

The leaven that would set my life in motion is absent; gone is the stimulus that kept me cheerful late at night, that roused me from sleep in the morning.

I have found only one congenial woman here, a Fräulein B . . . , she is like you, dear Lotte, if anyone can be like you. Ha! you will say, the man thinks up pretty compliments! And it is not entirely untrue. For some time I have been very well behaved because I can't be otherwise, I am quite witty, and the women say that no one knows how to praise as subtly as I (and to lie, they add, because without that it can't be brought off, do you understand?). I was starting to speak of Fräulein B . . . She has a fine soul, which shines forth brightly from her blue eyes. Her class is a burden to her that satisfies none of the desires of her heart. She longs to get away from all the bustle, and we pass many hours fantasizing about rural scenes of untrammeled happiness; and about you! How often must she pay tribute to you, not must, she does it willingly, is so glad to hear about you, loves you.—

Oh, if I were sitting at your feet in the dear, intimate little room, and our dear little ones were waltzing with one another around me, and if they got too loud for you I would gather them around and quiet them with a frightening fairy tale.

The sun is setting gloriously over the landscape, and its gleaming snow, the storm has passed, and I——must lock myself up in my cage again.—Adieu! Is Albert with you? And how——? God forgive me this question!

FEBRUARY 8

For the past eight days we have been having the most horrible weather, but it does me good. For as long as I have been here, no fine day has appeared in the sky that someone has not ruined or spoiled for me. But if it rains hard and blows and freezes and thaws: ha! I think, it can't be any worse at home than it is outside, or vice versa, and that's fine. If the sun comes up in the morning and promises a lovely day, I can never help exclaiming: Now they have another gift from heaven with which they can cheat one another. There is nothing they don't cheat one another about: health, a good name, cheerfulness, convalescence! And mostly from foolishness, obtuseness, and narrow-mindedness, even if you listen to them with the greatest indulgence. Sometimes I would like to beg them on my knees not to rage so furiously in their own innards.

FEBRUARY 17

I am afraid that my ambassador and I are not going to be together much longer. The man is absolutely unbearable.

The way he works and conducts business is so ridiculous that I can't prevent myself from contradicting him, and often do something according to my idea and in my way, which he, naturally, never accepts. He complained about me recently at Court, and the Minister gave me a rebuke that may have been gentle but was still a rebuke, and I was on the point of putting in for my resignation when I received a private letter* from him, a letter before which I knelt down and worshiped its high, noble, wise import. How he reprimanded my all too excessive feeling, how he honored as youthful courage my inflated notions of being effective, of influence on others, of getting through to others on matters of business. He wrote this not to root them out but only to mitigate them and attempt to lead them to where they could have their true play, their powerful effect. And for a week I was strengthened and at one with myself. Calmness of soul is a glorious thing, and joy in oneself. Dear friend, if only the precious stone were not just as fragile as it is beautiful and costly.

FEBRUARY 20

God bless you, my dear ones, and give you all the good days He strips away from me!

I thank you, Albert, for deceiving me: I was waiting for news when your wedding day would be, and had planned on that day to solemnly take down Lotte's silhouette from

---

*Out of respect for this excellent gentleman, the letter here referred to, and another to be mentioned later, have been withdrawn from this collection because it was not thought that such an audacity could be excused even by the warmest gratitude of the public. [Goethe's "editor's" note—trans.]

the wall and bury it under other papers. Now you are a couple and her image is still there! Well, let it stay! And why not? I know I am with you both too, am, without injuring you, in Lotte's heart, have, yes, have the second place in it and will and must maintain it. Oh, I would go mad if she could forget— Albert, a hell lies in the thought. Albert, farewell! Farewell, angel from heaven! Farewell, Lotte!

MARCH 15

I have had a vexation that will drive me away from here. It makes me grind my teeth! Damn! It can't be made good, and it's all your fault, all you who drove and tormented me and spurred me on to take a position that was against my inclination. This is what I get! This is what you get! And so you won't say again that my exaggerated ideas ruin everything, here, my dear sir, is a narration, plain and simple, as a chronicler would record it.

Count von C . . . loves me, honors me, that is well-known, I have written you that a hundred times. Yesterday I dined with him, it happened to be on the day the aristocratic society of ladies and gentlemen gathers at his house in the evening, which had never occurred to me, nor that we subordinates had no business there. Fine. I dine with the Count, and afterwards we walk up and down in the great hall; I am talking with him and with Colonel B . . . , who joins us, and the hour for the gathering draws near. God knows, I'm thinking nothing at all. Then overgracious Lady von S . . . enters with her Sir Spouse and well-hatched gosling daughter with the flat chest and sweet little beanpole body, widen *en passant* their ancestrally aristocratic eyes and nostrils, and as I despise the whole nation of them from the bottom of my heart, I was on the point of taking my leave and was only waiting for the Count to be free from the dreadful twaddle when my Fräulein B... entered. Since my heart always expands a little whenever I see her, I remained, placed myself behind her chair, and only after a while noticed that she was speaking to me with less openness than before, and with some embarrassment. That struck me. Is she too like all the rest, I thought, was hurt and about to leave, and yet I stayed because I would gladly have excused her, didn't believe it, still hoped for a good word from her, and—whatever you like. Meanwhile more people gathered. Baron F..., whose whole wardrobe dates from the era of the coronation of Franz the First; the Court Chancellor R..., here however formally addressed as Herr von R..., with his deaf wife et cetera, not to forget the badly turned out J..., who patches his old-Frankish wardrobe with new-style rags; the room fills up, and I am chatting with several of my acquaintances, who are all quite laconic. I thought—but was only paying attention to my Fräulein B... I did not notice that the women at the end of the room were whispering in each other's ears, that it was circulating among the men, that Frau von S... was speaking to the Count (Fräulein B... told me all this later), until finally the Count came up to me and took me aside in a window niche.—You know, he said, our peculiar customs; I notice that these people are displeased to see you here. I would not for anything want to— Your Excellency, I interrupted, I beg your pardon a thousand times. I should have thought of it before, and I know you will forgive me this indiscretion; I was about to take my leave earlier, an evil genius held me back, I added, smiling as I bowed.— The Count pressed my hand with a feeling that said everything. I softly slipped away from the aristocratic party, left,

got into a cabriolet, and rode to M . . . to watch the sun setting from the hill and meanwhile to read in my Homer the
wonderful passage about how Ulysses is welcomed and
cared for by the splendid swineherds. All that was good.

In the evening I came back for supper, there were still a
few people in the inn; they were casting dice on a corner of
the table, from which they had folded back the cloth. Then
honorable Adelin comes in, looks at me as he puts down
his hat, comes over to me, and says softly: You are upset?—
Me? I said.—The Count made you leave the party.—The
devil take them! I said, I was happy to get out into the open
air.—It's good, he said, that you take it lightly. But I'm
vexed that it's already all over the place.—Then the thing
really began to gnaw at me. All those who came to the table
and were looking at me, I thought, did so on that account!
That made for bad blood.

And since today as well, wherever I walk, people pity
me, since I hear that those who envy me are triumphant,
saying: You see what happens to the arrogant, who overrate
their little bit of intelligence and think it gives them the
right to set themselves above all the customs of society, and
more such dog twaddle—then one wants to plunge a dagger into one's heart; for one can say of independence what
one will, I would like to see the man who can endure having rogues talk about him when they have an advantage
over him. When their gossip is groundless, then one can
easily ignore it.

MARCH 16

Everything hounds me. Today I met Fräulein B . . . out
walking, I couldn't refrain from addressing her, and as soon

as we were away from people, expressing my hurt at her recent behavior.—O Werther, she said in a heartfelt tone, how could you interpret my confusion like that, since you know my heart? What I suffered on your account, from the moment I entered the room! I foresaw it all, it was on the tip of my tongue a hundred times to tell you, that Frau von S . . . and Frau von T . . . and their husbands would sooner leave than remain in your company. I knew that the Count could not risk offending them—and now the uproar!— What, Fräulein? I said, concealing my shock, for at this moment everything Adelin had told me the day before yesterday ran through my veins like boiling water.—How much it has already cost me! the sweet creature said, with tears in her eyes.—I was no longer master of myself, was on the point of throwing myself at her feet.—Explain yourself, I cried.—The tears rolled down her cheeks. I was beside myself. She dried them without trying to conceal them.—You know my aunt, she began. She was there and saw it, and oh, with what eyes! Werther, what a sermon I had to endure last night and this morning about my association with you, and I had to listen to your being denigrated, humiliated, and could not and was not allowed to even halfway defend you.

Every word she spoke went through my heart like a sword. She did not feel what a mercy it would have been to keep all that from me; and now on top of it she added what more would be gossiped about, what kind of people would exult over it. How they would be tickled and delighted about the punishment for my arrogance and my belittling of others, which they had long held against me. To hear all that from her, Wilhelm, in a voice of the most genuine sympathy—I was devastated, and am still raging inside. I wanted one person to dare reproach me so I could drive a dagger through his body; if I could see blood I would feel better. Oh, I have grabbed a knife a hundred times to ease this oppressed heart! They tell of a noble race of horses that, when they are terribly driven and overheated, instinctively bite open a vein to help themselves breathe. I often feel that way, I would like to open one of my veins, to bring me eternal freedom.

MARCH 24

I have requested my dismissal from Court and will, I hope, receive it, and you will all pardon me for not first getting your permission. I just had to get away, and I know everything you have to say to talk me into staying, and so—tell my mother gently; I cannot help myself, and she will just have to accept that I can't help her either. Of course she will be hurt. To see the fine career that her son was just beginning, leading to privy councillor and ambassador, suddenly brought to a halt and back into its stall with the little beast! Make of it what you all will, and argue about the possible circumstances in which I might and ought to have stayed; enough, I'm leaving, and so that you know where I'm going, there is a Prince *** here who takes great pleasure in my company; he asked me, when he heard my intention, to go with him to his estate and spend the lovely spring there. I am to be left entirely to myself, he promised, and since we understand each other up to a point, I will trust to luck and go with him.

Thanks for both your letters. I didn't reply because I let my letter lie until I had received permission to leave Court; I was afraid my mother would appeal to the Minister and interfere with my intention. But now it has happened, my permission has arrived. I don't need to tell all of you how reluctantly it was granted, and what the Minister writes: you would break out in fresh lamentations. The Crown Prince sent me a present of twenty-five ducats, with a note that moved me to tears, so I don't need the money from my mother I recently wrote for.

MAY 5

I'm leaving here tomorrow, and because my birthplace is only six miles out of my way I want to see it again, want to call to mind the old days that I happily dreamed away. I will enter by the same gate through which my mother rode out with me when she left the dear place after my father's death to lock herself up in her unbearable town. Adieu, Wilhelm, you will hear of my progress.

MAY 9

I have completed the pilgrimage to my hometown with all a pilgrim's devotion, and have been overcome by many unexpected feelings. I had the coach stop at the great linden tree that stands a quarter of an hour before the town in the direction of S . . . , got out, and bade the postilion go on, in

order to taste on foot to my heart's content every newly re-
vived and vivid memory. There I stood under the linden,
which, when I was a boy, had been the goal and boundary
of my walks. How different now! At that time, in happy ig-
norance, I longed to go out into the unknown world, where
I hoped for so much nourishment for my heart, so much
enjoyment, to fill and satisfy my longing, striving breast.
Now I return from the wide world—O my friend, with
how many shattered hopes, with how many thwarted
plans!—I saw lying before me the hills that so many thousand times had been the object of my desires. I could sit
here for hours and look over at them, with fervent soul lose
myself in the woods and valleys that presented themselves
to my eyes in such hazy, friendly fashion, and when the
hour came when I had to return, with what reluctance did
I not leave the dear spot!—I approached the town, greeted
all the old, well-known garden sheds, the new ones re-
pelled me, as did all the other changes that had been made.
I entered the town gate and found myself again completely
and at once. Dear friend, I don't want to go into detail; as
charming as I found it, it would be monotonous in the telling. I had decided to stay on the market square, right beside
our old house. On the way there I noticed that the school-
room into which an honorable old woman had crammed
our childhood had been turned into a notions shop. I remembered the restlessness, the tears, the apathy, the profound anxiety I had endured in that hole.—I did not take a
step that was not extraordinary. A pilgrim in the Holy Land
does not come upon as many places of religious memories,
and his soul is hardly as full of sacred emotion.—Another
detail, in place of many: I walked along the river to a certain
farm, that used to be my usual path, and to the little spot

where we boys practiced who could skip the most flat stones on the water. I remember so vividly sometimes standing there and watching the water flow past, and with what magic presentiments I followed it, how adventuresome I imagined the places to be it was flowing to, and how I so soon discovered limits to my powers of imagination, and yet had to go on, further and further, until I had totally lost myself in the contemplation of invisible distances.—You see, my friend, so limited and happy were the glorious fathers of old, so childlike their feeling, their poetry! When Ulysses speaks of the unmeasured sea and the infinite earth, that is so true, so human, heartfelt, limited, and mysterious. What good does it do me to be able to repeat with every schoolboy that the earth is round? A person needs only a few clumps of earth to enjoy himself on it, fewer still to rest beneath it.

Now I am here at the Prince's hunting lodge. Being with him is rather pleasant, he is simple and genuine. There are odd people around him whom I can't figure out at all. They don't seem to be rogues, and yet they don't have the look of honest people, either. Sometimes they seem to me to be honorable, but still I can't trust them. What I regret is that he often speaks of matters he has only heard or read about, and always from the point of view that someone has presented to him.

Then too, he esteems my understanding and talents more than he does this heart that is my only pride, that all by itself is the source of everything, of all energy, all happiness, and all misery. What I know anyone can know—my heart is mine alone.

I had been thinking of something I didn't want to tell you about until I had done it; now that nothing will come of it, it's just as well. I wanted to join the war; it had long been dear to my heart. That's the main reason I followed the Prince here; he is a General in the ***'s service. On a walk I revealed my purpose to him; he advised me against it, and it would have had to be more passion than caprice on my part if I had not been willing to listen to his reasons.

Say what you will, I can't stay here any longer. What is there here for me? The time drags. The Prince treats me as well as possible, and yet I am not in my own situation. We have at bottom nothing in common with each other. He is a man of understanding, but of quite common understanding; being in his company entertains me no more than reading a well-written book. I'll stay another week, and then wander around aimlessly again. The best thing I have done here is my sketching. The Prince has a feeling for art and would have an even stronger feeling for it if he were not limited by the dreadful strictures of criticism and its humdrum terminology. Sometimes I grind my teeth when I warmly guide him through nature and art with my imagination and he thinks he suddenly understands it really well, but then he stumbles onto some trite art term.

JUNE 16

Yes, I am surely a wanderer, a pilgrim on earth. Are any of you more?

JUNE 18

Where do I want to go? That can be revealed to you in confidence. I must stay here for another two weeks, and then I fooled myself into thinking I wanted to visit the mines in ***; but of course there is nothing to it, I only want to be closer to Lotte again, that is all. I laugh at my own heart—and do its will.

JULY 29

No, it is well! Everything is well!—I—her husband! O God who made me, if you had prepared me for this blessedness my whole life would be a lasting prayer. I don't want to argue, and pardon me these tears, pardon my vain desires!—She my wife! If I had embraced in my arms the dearest creature under the sun—a shudder runs through my whole body, Wilhelm, when Albert grasps her around her slender waist.

And may I say it? Why not, Wilhelm? She would have been happier with me than with him. He is not the man to fulfill all the desires of her heart. A certain lack of sensitive perception, a lack—take it as you will, that his heart does not beat in sympathy with—oh!—with the place in a dear book where my heart and Lotte's meet as one; in a hundred other incidents when it happens that our feelings about some action of a third person find expression. Dear Wilhelm!—To be sure, he loves her with all his soul, and how should she not deserve such a love!

An unbearable person has interrupted me. My tears are dried. I am distracted. Adieu, dear friend!

AUGUST 4

It doesn't happen just with me. Everyone is deceived in his hopes, cheated in his expectations. I visited my good woman under the linden trees. The oldest boy ran up to me, his cries of joy brought the mother, who looked quite despondent. Her first words were: Good sir, alas, my Hans has died!—He was the youngest of her boys. I was silent.— And my husband, she said, has come back from Switzerland bringing nothing, and without some good people he would have had to beg his way back, he got a fever on the journey.—I was unable to say anything to her and gave the little one something, she asked me to accept a few apples, which I did, and left the place of sad memory.

AUGUST 21

I keep changing, the way one turns over one's hand. Sometimes a joyous ray of life will gleam up again, but alas! only for a moment!—When I lose myself in dreams this way I cannot help thinking: What if Albert were to die? You would! Yes, she would—and then I chase after the will-o'-the-wisp until it leads me to abysses before which I draw back trembling.

When I go out through the town gate, the way I took the first time to fetch Lotte for the dance, how completely different it was! Everything, everything, has passed on! No hint of the previous world, no pulse-beat of my former feelings. I feel as a ghost must feel returning to a destroyed, burnt-out castle he had once built as a radiant prince, furnished with all the gifts of glory that, dying, he had, full of hope, bequeathed to his beloved son.

SEPTEMBER 3

Sometimes I don't understand how another can love her, is allowed to love her, since I love her so completely myself, so intensely, so fully, grasp nothing, know nothing, have nothing but her!

SEPTEMBER 4

Yes, so it is. As nature draws on to autumn, it is becoming autumn in me and around me. My leaves are turning yellow, and the leaves of the neighboring trees have already fallen. Didn't I write you about a peasant lad, right after I came here? I recently inquired after him again in Wahlheim; it seems he was dismissed and no one wanted to have anything more to do with him. Yesterday by chance I ran into him on the way to another village. I greeted him, and he told me his story, which doubly and triply moved me, as you will easily understand when I relate it to you. But what good is all that? Why don't I keep for myself what frightens and upsets me? Why sadden you? Why do I always give you reason to feel sorry for me and scold me? Well, so be it, that too might be part of my fate!

The man began to answer my questions with a quiet sadness in which I seemed to notice something of a shy nature, but quite soon more openly, as if he were recognizing again both himself and me. He confessed his errors to me, lamented his misfortune. If I could present each of his words to you, my friend, before the bar of justice! He confessed, indeed he explained with a kind of enjoyment and happiness in recalling the memory, that his passion for the housewife had increased daily, that finally he no longer knew what he was doing, what he was saying, where his head had got to. He was not able to eat or drink or sleep, his throat constricted, he did what he ought not to have done, what he was ordered to do he forgot; he was as if pursued by an evil spirit, until one day, when he knew she was in an upstairs room, he went after her, or rather he was drawn to go to her; since she paid no attention to his pleadings he tried to overcome her by force, he didn't know what was happening to him, God was his witness that his intentions toward her had always been honorable, and that he wished for nothing more devoutly than that she should marry him, that she would spend her life with him. After he had spoken for a while he began to hesitate, like one who still has something to say but doesn't trust himself to get it out; finally he confessed to me, also shyly, what small intimacies she had permitted him, and what closeness she would allow him. He broke off twice, three times, and repeated the most earnest protestations that he wasn't saying that to make her look bad, as he expressed himself, but that he loved and esteemed her as before, that such a thing would never come from his mouth, and that he was only telling it to me to convince me that he was not a completely perverse and dreadful person.—And here, my dear friend, I begin again with my old song that I will strike up eternally: If I could show you the man as he stood before me, as he still stands before me! If I could tell you everything properly so that you would feel how I partake, must partake, of his destiny! But enough, since you know me and my destiny you know only too well what draws me to every unfortunate person, what draws me especially to this one.

As I read the page over again I see that I have forgotten to tell you the end of the story, which is easy to imagine. She warded him off; her brother, who had long hated him, intervened; he had long wanted the man out of the house because he feared that if his sister remarried his children would be deprived of the inheritance that now, since she is childless, gives them great hopes; the brother promptly threw him out of the house and made such a fuss about the matter that the woman could not have taken him back even if she had wanted to. Now she has hired another farmhand; about him too, it is said, she has had a falling-out with her brother, and it is asserted for a certainty that she will marry him; but my fellow is firmly resolved not to experience that.

What I am telling you is not exaggerated, in no way embroidered, indeed I can well say I have told it weakly, weakly, weakly, and coarsened it by relating it in our words of time-honored morality.

So this love, this faithfulness, this passion, is no poetic invention. It is alive, is at its most pure in the class of people we call uncultured, crude. We educated ones—miseducated to nothing! Read this story with reverence, I beg you. Today I am calm as I write it down; you can see from my hand that I'm not fussing and fuming as I usually do. Read it, my dear friend, and as you read think that it is also the story of your friend. Yes, so it has gone with me, so it will go, and I am not half so good, half so resolute as the poor unfortunate with whom I hardly dare compare myself.

SEPTEMBER 5

She had written a note to her husband, who was staying in the countryside on some business. It began: Dearest, best, beloved, come back, as soon as you can, I await you with a thousand joys.—A friend who came in brought the news that because of certain circumstances Albert would not be returning so soon. The note was left lying around, and fell into my hands that evening. I read it and smiled; she asked, what about?—What a gift of the gods the power of imagination is, I exclaimed, I could delude myself for a moment that it had been written to me.—She broke off, it seemed to displease her, and I was silent.

SEPTEMBER 6

With great difficulty I have finally decided to lay by the simple blue coat in which I danced with Lotte for the first time, it had by now become unpresentable. I had another one made exactly like its predecessor in collar and sleeve, and also the same yellow vest and trousers.

But somehow it doesn't have quite the same effect. I don't know—I think I will get attached to it with time.

SEPTEMBER 12

She was away for a few days to fetch Albert. Today I entered her room, she came toward me, and I kissed her hand with a thousand joys.

A canary flew from the mirror onto her shoulder.——A new friend, she said, and coaxed it onto her hand. He is intended for my little ones. He is so dear! Look at him! When I give him bread he flutters his wings and pecks so charmingly. He kisses me too, look!

As she held the small creature to her mouth, it pressed itself so captivatingly on those sweet lips, as if it could have felt the happiness it was enjoying.

He shall kiss you too, she said, and handed the bird over to me.——The little beak made its way from her lips to mine, and the pecking touch was like a breath, an intimation, of loving enjoyment.

Its kiss, I said, is not entirely without desire, it is seeking food and withdrawing dissatisfied from the empty caress.

He eats from my mouth, too, she said.——She offered it a few crumbs with her lips, from which the joys of innocently devoted love smiled in complete bliss.

I turned my face away. She should not do this! Not fire up my imagination with these images of divine innocence and happiness, not wake my heart from the sleep in which it is sometimes cradled by the indifference of life!——But why not?——She trusts me so! She knows how I love her!

SEPTEMBER 15

It can drive one mad, Wilhelm, that there should be people who have no idea or feeling for the few things on earth that are still worth something. You know the walnut trees beneath which I sat with Lotte at the honorable pastor's in St . . . , the glorious walnut trees which, God knows, always filled my soul with the greatest delight! How intimate they made the yard of the parsonage, how cooling! And how magnificent the branches were! And remembering them back to the honest clerics who planted them so many years ago. The schoolmaster had often recalled for us one name that he had heard from his grandfather; he was said to be such a good man, and his memory was always sacred to me beneath the trees. I tell you, the schoolmaster had tears in his eyes as we spoke yesterday about how they had been hacked down.—Hacked down! I could fly into a rage, murder the dog that struck the first blow! I, who if such trees stood in my yard and one of them should die of old age, could grieve that I would have to look on. Dear friend! There is one consolation! That there is human feeling! The whole village is grumbling, and I hope the pastor's wife will feel in butter and eggs and other confidences what kind of wound she has given her village. For she it is, the wife of the new pastor (our old one has died), a gaunt, sickly creature who has very good reason not to take part in the world, for no one wants any part of her. A fool who passes herself off as learned, busies herself with investigations into the canon, labors a good deal on the newfangled moral-critical reformation of Christianity, and shrugs her shoulders at Lavater's effusions. Her health is shattered, and because of that she finds no joy on God's earth. Only such a creature was capable of cutting down my walnut trees. As you see, I can't get over it! Just think, she thought the falling leaves made the courtyard dirty and moldy, the trees robbed her of light, and when the nuts were ripe the boys would throw stones at them, and that got on her nerves, that disturbed her deep reflections when she was weighing Kennicot, Semler, and Michaelis against each other. When I saw how upset the villagers were, especially the old people, I said to them: Why did you let it happen?—Around here, if it's what the mayor wants, what can one do?—But one good thing happened: the mayor and the pastor, who wanted to have some advantage from his wife's whims, which in any case weren't putting any fat in his soup, thought of dividing the trees between them. But the Council got wind of it and said: They're ours! For it still had an old claim to the part of the parson's yard where the trees stood, and sold them to the highest bidder. They are down! Oh, if I were a prince! I would put the pastor's wife, the mayor, and the Council—prince!—ha, but if I were a prince, what would I care about the trees in my country?

OCTOBER 10

Just looking into her black eyes makes me happy! But what vexes me is that Albert does not seem to be as delighted as he—hoped—as I—thought I was—when—I don't like to use dashes, but here I can't express myself any other way—and, I think, clearly enough.

OCTOBER 12

Ossian has displaced Homer in my heart. What a world this glorious poet opens up for me! To wander over the heath with the storm winds roaring around me, winds leading on the ghosts of the ancient fathers in the streaming fog by the fitful light of the moon. To hear coming from the mountains, half blown away by the roaring of the forest stream, the moaning of spirits from their caves, and the lamentations of the girl grieving herself to death around the four moss-covered stones of the noble warrior fallen in battle, her beloved. When I come upon the wandering gray bard, seeking over the vast heath the footsteps of his ancestors and oh! finding their gravestones and then looking, wailing, up to the dear stars of the evening that hides itself in the roiling sea, and the ages of the past come alive in the hero's soul, those times when the friendly ray illumined the dangers of the brave, and the moon shone on their laurel-crowned victorious ship returning. When I read the profound grief on his brow, see this last, abandoned, glorious man tottering exhausted to the grave, how he continually sucks in new, painfully glowing joys in the feeble presence of the shades of his departed ones and looks down at the cold earth, the high, waving grasses, and calls out: The wanderer who knew me in my prime will come, come, and ask: Where is the singer, Fingal's splendid son? His step passes over my grave, and he asks after me in vain on this earth.— O friend! I would wish like a noble bearer of arms to draw my sword to free my prince at once from the flickering pain of his slowly departing life, and send my soul after the liberated demigod.

OCTOBER 19

Oh, this hole, this enormous, horrible hole I feel here in my breast!—I often think, if you could press her just once, just once, to this heart, this hole would be completely filled.

OCTOBER 26

Yes, I am certain, my friend, certain and ever more certain that a creature's existence matters little, very little. One of her friends came to Lotte, and I went into the adjoining room to take up a book but couldn't read, and took up a pen to write. I heard them talking softly; they were telling each other insignificant things, news of the town: how this woman married, how that one is ill, very ill—she has a dry cough, the bones are standing out in her face, and she has fainting fits; I wouldn't put a penny on her life, one of them said.—Mr. X is also in a bad way, Lotte said.—He is swollen, the other replied.—And my vivid imagination transported me to the beds of these poor creatures; I saw them, saw how reluctantly they turned their backs on life, how they— Wilhelm! and my little women were talking about it the way one talks about it—that a stranger dies.—And when I look around the room, and see around me Lotte's clothes and Albert's writings and this furniture with which I am so familiar, even this inkwell, and think: See what you are to this house! Everything! Your friends honor you! You often make their joy, and it seems to your heart that it could not exist without them; and yet—if you were now to leave, to part from this circle? Would they, how long would they feel the gap that losing you tore in their destiny? How long?— Oh, man is so transient that even where he is really certain of his existence, even where he makes the one true impression of his presence, in the memory, in the soul of his dear ones, even there must he disappear, be extinguished, and that so soon!

OCTOBER 27

Often I would like to tear my breast and batter my brain that we can mean so little to each other. Oh, the love, joy, warmth, and bliss that I don't bring to others, others will not give to me, but even with a heart filled with happiness I will not be able to make happy a person who stands cold and inert before me.

OCTOBER 27, EVENING

I have so much, and my feeling for her swallows up everything. I have so much, but without her everything becomes nothing.

OCTOBER 30

If I haven't a hundred times been on the point of falling on her breast! God knows how one feels seeing so much amiability displayed in front of one and not being allowed to reach out for it; yet reaching out is the most natural drive of mankind. Don't children reach out for everything that catches their attention?—And I?

NOVEMBER 3

God knows, I often lie down to sleep with the desire, even sometimes the hope, not to wake up again; and in the morning I open my eyes, see the sun again, and am miserable. Oh, if I could be moody, blame it on the weather, on a third person, on a miscarried undertaking, then the unbearable burden of aimlessness would weigh on me only half as much. Alas! I feel only too keenly that the fault lies with me alone—not fault! The source of all misery lies concealed within me, as the source of all happiness did formerly. Am I not still the same person who used to drift around in all the fullness of feeling, whom a paradise followed at every step, who had a heart able to lovingly encompass an entire world? But this heart is now dead, from it flow no more delights, my eyes are dry, and my senses, no longer laved by refreshing tears, anxiously furrow my brow. I suffer a great deal, for I have lost what was my life's sole bliss, the sacred, invigorating power with which I created worlds around me. It is no more!—When I look out my window at the distant hill, at how the morning sun breaks through the fog above it and shines on the quiet meadowland and the gentle river snaking its way toward me between its leafless willows—Oh! When this glorious nature lies before me as stiffly as a lacquered miniature, and all its bliss cannot pump from my heart to my brain a single drop of happiness, and this whole fellow stands before God's countenance like a stopped-up well, like a leaky bucket. I have often thrown myself on the floor and begged God for tears like a husbandman for rain when the sky above him is brass and the earth thirsting around him.

But oh! I feel how God gives rain and sunshine not according to our importunate prayers, and those times whose memories torment me, why else were they so blessed than because I waited patiently for His spirit, and received the bliss that He showered on me with my whole, fervently thankful heart!

She has reproached me for my excesses! Ah, with such amiability! My excesses, that I sometimes let myself be induced
by a glass of wine to drink a whole bottle.—Don't! she said.
Think of Lotte!—Think, I said, do you need to tell me to
do that? I think!—I don't think! You are always before my
soul. Today I was sitting at the spot where you recently got
down from the coach— She changed the subject to keep
me from going on any further. Dear friend! I am lost! She
can do with me what she will.

I thank you, Wilhelm, for your heartfelt sympathy, for your
well-intentioned advice, but beg you to be quiet. Let me
stick it out. Blessedly exhausted as I am, I have strength
enough to carry through. I honor religion, you know that, I
feel it is a staff for many weary souls, refreshment for many
a one who is pining away. But—can it, must it, be the same
thing for everyone? If you look at the great world, you see
thousands for whom it wasn't, thousands for whom it will
not be the same, preached or unpreached, and must it then
be the same for me? Does not the son of God Himself say
that those would be around Him whom the Father had
given Him? But if I am not given? If the Father wants to
keep me for Himself, as my heart tells me?—I beg you, do
not misinterpret this, do not see mockery in these innocent
words. What I am laying before you is my whole soul;
otherwise I would rather have kept silent, as I do not like to
lose words over things that everyone knows as little about

as I do. What else is it but human destiny to suffer out one's measure, drink up one's cup?—And if the chalice was too bitter for the God from heaven on His human lips, why should I boast and pretend that it tastes sweet to me? And why should I be ashamed in the terrible moment when my entire being trembles between being and nothingness, since the past flashes like lightning above the dark abyss of the future and everything around me is swallowed up, and the world perishes with me?—Is that not the voice of the creature thrown back on itself, failing, trapped, lost, and inexorably tumbling downward, the voice groaning in the inner depths of its vainly upwards-struggling energies: My God! My God! Why hast thou forsaken me? And if I should be ashamed of the expression, should I be afraid when facing that moment, since it did not escape Him who rolls up heaven like a carpet?

NOVEMBER 21

She doesn't see, doesn't feel, that she is preparing a poison that will destroy both her and me; and I lustfully drain the cup she hands me for my ruin. Why the kindly glance with which she often—often?—no, not often, but sometimes looks at me, the obligingness with which she responds to an involuntary expression of my feeling, the compassion with which she bears with me, compassion I see on her brow?

Yesterday, as I was leaving, she held out her hand to me and said: Adieu, dear Werther!—Dear Werther! It was the first time she called me "dear," and it went through me heart and soul. I repeated it to myself a hundred times, and last night, as I was about to go to bed and was chattering to myself about all sorts of things, I suddenly said: Good night, dear Werther! and then had to laugh at myself.

I cannot pray: Leave her to me! and yet I often think of her as mine. I cannot pray: Give her to me! for she is another's. I jest with my pains; if I were to let myself go there would be a whole litany of antitheses.

She feels what I am suffering. Today her glance plunged deep into my heart. I found her alone; I said nothing, and she looked at me. And I no longer saw in her the sweet beauty, the glow of her splendid spirit, it had all disappeared before my eyes. A far more glorious look affected me, full of the most heartfelt concern, the sweetest sympathy. Why was I not permitted to throw myself at her feet? Why could I not answer by embracing her with a thousand kisses? She took refuge at the clavier, and in a soft, sweet voice breathed harmonious sounds as she played. Never have I seen her lips so charming; it was as if they opened, thirsting to drink in the sweet tones welling up out of the instrument, and it was only their secret echo resounding from her pure mouth—Oh, if I were able to describe it to you!—I resisted no longer, bowed, and swore: I will never dare press a kiss on you, O lips above which the spirits of heaven hover—and yet—I want—Ha! You see, it stands before my soul like a dividing wall—this blessedness—and then perished to atone for this sin.—Sin?

Sometimes I tell myself: Your fate is unique; count the others happy—no other person has ever been as tormented. Then I read a poet from primitive times, and it seems as if I were looking into my own heart. I have to endure so much! Have people before me been so miserable?

I cannot, I cannot get hold of myself! Wherever I step I am met with a vision that completely upsets me. Today! O fate! O humanity!

I was walking along the water at the noon hour, I had no desire to eat. Everything was desolate, a cold, damp west wind was blowing from the mountain, and gray rain clouds were drawing into the valley. From a distance I saw a person in a shabby green coat scrambling around among the rocks, who appeared to be looking for herbs. As I came nearer to him and he turned around at the noise I made, I saw a most interesting face, whose outstanding trait was a quiet grief, but which otherwise expressed nothing but simple good sense. His black hair had been put up in two rolls with pins and the remainder woven into a heavy pigtail that hung down his back. As his clothing seemed to indicate a person of humble class, I thought he would not take it amiss if I were curious about what he was doing, and so I asked him what was he looking for.—I'm seeking flowers, he answered with a deep sigh, but find none.—But it is not the season, I said, smiling. There are so many flowers, he said as he came down to me. Out in my garden are roses and two kinds of honeysuckle, one my father gave me; they grow like weeds; I've been looking for them for two days but can't find them. Out there too there are always flowers, yellow and blue and red, and the feverwort has a pretty little flower. I can't find any of them.—I noticed something odd, and so I asked him in a roundabout way: What do you want with the flowers?—A strange, twitching smile spread over his face.—If you won't betray me, he said, pressing a finger to his lips, I have promised my sweetheart a bouquet.—That is good of you, I said.—Oh, he said, she has many other things, she is rich.—And yet she will cherish your bouquet, I replied.—Oh! he went on, she has jewels and a crown.—What is her name?—If the States General were to pay me, he responded, I would be another person! Yes, there was once a time when I was so happy! Now it's over with me. I am now—a damp glance at the sky expressed everything.—So you were happy? I asked.—Oh, I wish I were again! he said. Then I felt so happy, so merry, as light as a fish in water!—Heinrich! an old woman coming up the path called out, Heinrich, where have you got to? We've been looking for you everywhere. Come to supper!—Is that your son? I asked, going up to her. Indeed, my poor son! she replied. God has laid a heavy burden upon me. How long has he been like this? I asked.—So peaceful, she said, for half a year now. Thank God he has come this far, before he was raving for a whole year, chained up in a madhouse. Now he doesn't bother anyone but is always treating with kings and emperors. He was such a good, quiet person, he helped support me, wrote a fine hand, and suddenly he became absorbed, fell into a violent fever, from that into a frenzy, and now he is as you see him. If I were to tell you, sir— I interrupted the stream of her words with the question: What sort of time was it that he boasts he was so happy in?—The foolish man! she exclaimed with a sympathetic smile, he means the time when he was out of his mind, he always boasts about that; that's the time he was in the madhouse, when he knew nothing of himself.—That struck me like a thunderclap; I pressed a coin into her hand and quickly left her.

When you were happy! I exclaimed to myself, walking rapidly toward the town, when you were as happy as a fish in water!—Dear God! Have you made that the destiny of men, that they are not happy except before they attain reason and after they lose it again!—Miserable man!—And how I also envy you your melancholy, the confusion of your senses in which you are pining away! You go out full of hope to pick flowers for your queen—in winter—and grieve when you don't find any, and do not understand why you cannot find them. And I—I go out without hope, without purpose, and return home as I left it.—You imagine what a person you would be if the States General were to pay you. Blessed creature, that can ascribe his want of happiness to an earthly obstacle! You do not feel! You do not feel that your misery lies in your shattered heart, in your ruined brain, a misery that all the kings on earth cannot help you with.

Must he die without hope who ridicules a sick person who travels to the most distant spring that will worsen his disease, will make his fading away more painful? Who elevates himself above his oppressed heart which, to be rid of the pangs of conscience and cast off the sufferings of his soul, makes a pilgrimage to the sacred tomb? Every step that the soles of his feet cut through unmarked paths is a drop of balm for the tortured soul, and after every day that he has held out on his journey his heart lays itself down eased of much distress. And you call that madness, you word grubbers on your cushions?—Madness!—O God! You see my tears! Did You, who created man poor enough, also have to give him brothers who rob him of the little bit of poverty, the little bit of faith that he has in You, in You, the Ever-loving! For belief in a healing root, in the tears of the vine, what else is it but confidence in You, that You have put healing and soothing power, of which we have need every hour, in everything around us? Father! Whom I do not know! Father! who filled all my soul and who has now turned His countenance away from me! Call me to You! Be silent no longer! Your silence will not stay this thirsting soul—and could a person, a father, be angry whose son, unexpectedly returning, threw himself on his neck and cried: Father! I have come back! Don't be angry that I am breaking off the travels that you meant for me to endure longer. The world is everywhere the same, in effort and work, reward and joy, but what is that to me? I am only happy where you are, and it is before your countenance that I want to suffer and enjoy.—And You, dear heavenly Father, would turn him away from You?

DECEMBER 1

Wilhelm! The person I wrote you about, the happy unfortunate, was a clerk of Lotte's father, and it was a passion for her, which he nourished, concealed, revealed, and for which he was dismissed, that drove him mad. Feel in these dry words with what agitation this story seized me. Albert told it to me just as calmly as you will perhaps read it.

DECEMBER 4

I beg you—look, I can't go on, I can't bear it any longer! Today I was sitting by her—sitting, she was playing on her clavier, different melodies, and all that expression! All!— All!—What could I— Her little sister was grooming her doll on my knee. Tears came to my eyes. I bent down, and saw her wedding ring.—My tears flowed—and suddenly she took up that old, divinely sweet melody, so suddenly, and through my soul went a feeling of consolation and a memory of what had passed, of the times I had heard the song, of the gloomy periods, the vexation, the thwarted hopes, and then—I paced up and down the room, my heart was suffocating under the provocation.—For God's sake, I said, turning on her with a fierce outburst, for God's sake, stop!—She stopped, and stared fixedly at me.—Werther, she said with a smile that went through my soul, Werther, you are quite ill, you dislike your favorite dishes. Go, I beg you, calm yourself.—I tore myself away from her, and—God! You see my misery and will end it.

DECEMBER 6

How her form pursues me! Waking and dreaming it fills my entire soul! Here, when I close my eyes, here behind my forehead, where the powers of inner sight fuse, stand her black eyes. Here! I can't find words for it. If I close my eyes they are there: like a sea, like an abyss they lie before me, in me, fill the senses of my mind.

What is man, the touted demigod! Does he not lack powers just where he needs them most? And if he soars in joy or sinks in sorrow, isn't he in both brought to a halt by his cold, impassive consciousness, just when he longs to lose himself in the fullness of the infinite?

THE EDITOR TO
THE READER

How I wish that enough original documents remained concerning the remarkable last days of our friend so I would not have found it necessary to interrupt with narrative the sequence of letters he left behind.

I have concerned myself with collecting precise information from the mouths of those who might be well acquainted with his story: it is a simple one, and with the exception of a few details all accounts are in agreement. There is only division of opinion and divergence of judgment regarding the state of mind of the people involved.

What else remains for us but to narrate conscientiously what we have been able to ascertain by repeated effort, to incorporate the letters left behind by the departed, and not to ignore the smallest retrieved paper, especially considering how difficult it is to uncover the motivating force of even a single action when it occurs among people who are not of the common sort.

Distress and lack of purpose had struck ever deeper root in Werther's soul, become ever more firmly entwined, and had gradually taken hold of his entire being. The harmony of his mind was completely shattered; an inner heat and intensity that permeated all the powers of his nature produced the most adverse effects and finally left him in a state of exhaustion from which he struggled more fearfully to emerge than he had struggled with all his previous troubles. The anxiety in his heart consumed all the other energies of his spirit, his vivacity, his astuteness; he became a sad presence in company, ever more unhappy and unjust the unhappier he became. At least this is what Albert's friends say. They maintain that Werther was unfair to a calm, pure man who had attained a long-desired happiness and acted to preserve this happiness into the future as well; Werther, who every day consumed his entire property only to suffer and have to pinch and scrape in the evening. Albert, they say, had not changed in such a short time, he was still the same person Werther had from the beginning known, honored, and esteemed. Albert loved Lotte above all, was proud of her and wished to see her recognized by everyone as the most wonderful creature. Was it to be held against him if he wished to turn away any appearance of suspicion, having no desire to share this precious possession, even in the most innocent fashion? They concede that Albert often left his wife's room when Werther was there, not from hatred or dislike of his friend but because he felt that Werther was depressed by his presence.

Lotte's father was taken with an illness that kept him confined to his room. He sent his coach for her, and she rode out. It was a lovely winter day; the first snow had fallen heavily and covered the whole region.

Werther followed the next morning, to take her home if Albert should not come to fetch her.

The clear weather could have small effect on his gloomy mind. A numbing weight lay on his soul, mournful images had taken firm hold of him, and his mind could only move from one painful thought to another.

As he lived in everlasting dissatisfaction with himself, the condition of others too seemed to him only more dubious and confused. He was convinced he had disturbed the beautiful relationship between Albert and his wife and reproached himself for it, reproaches mixed with a secret indignation against the husband.

On the way, his thoughts turned to this subject. Yes, yes, he said to himself, secretly gnashing his teeth: that's his amicable, tender, intimate involvement in everything; that's his calm, steady faithfulness! It's complacency and indifference! Doesn't every miserable piece of business attract him more than his dear, precious wife? Does he know how to appreciate his good fortune? Does he know how to respect her as she deserves? She is his, very well, she is his—I know that, and I know something else, too: I believe I've accustomed myself to the thought that will drive me mad, that will kill me yet.—And has his friendship for me lasted? Does he not see in my devotion to Lotte an interference with his rights, in my attentions to her a silent reproach? I am well aware, I feel it, that he is not glad to see me, he wishes me away, my presence is burdensome to him.

Werther often interrupted his rapid pace, stopped, and seemed to want to turn around; but again and again he directed his steps forward, and with these thoughts and inner conversations finally arrived, against his will so to speak, at the hunting lodge.

He came in the door, asked after the old man and Lotte, but found the house in some commotion. The oldest boy told him that a misfortune had happened over in Wahlheim, a peasant had been murdered!—This did not make any particular impression on him.—He stepped into the room and found Lotte busy convincing the old man, who despite his illness wanted to go to Wahlheim to investigate the deed on the spot. The murderer was still unknown, the dead man had been found in the morning in front of the door of his house, one had suspicions: the victim was the farmhand of a widow. She had previously had another in her service, who had left the house after a quarrel.

When Werther heard this he started violently.—Is it possible! he exclaimed, I must go there, I can't delay for an instant.—He hastened to Wahlheim with vivid memories, not doubting for an instant that the man he had spoken to several times and had taken a liking to had committed the deed.

As he had to pass by the linden trees to reach the inn where they had laid out the body, he was horrified by the square he had loved so much. The threshold on which the children of the neighborhood had so often played was besmirched with blood. Love and faithfulness, the most beautiful human feelings, had transformed themselves into violence and murder. The mighty trees stood leafless and white with frost, the lovely hedges that curled over the low cemetery wall had lost their leaves, and the gravestones, covered with snow, peeked through the gaps.

As he neared the inn, before which the whole village was gathered, a cry suddenly arose. From afar a troop of armed men was descried, and everyone shouted that the murderer was being brought in. Werther looked in that direction and did not long remain in doubt. Yes! it was the farmhand who so loved the widow, the man he had met some time ago who had been walking around in quiet grief, in secret despair.

What have you done, wretch! Werther shouted, running up to the prisoner.—The man looked at him coolly, was silent, and at last replied quite calmly: No one will have her, she will have no one.—They took the prisoner into the inn, and Werther hurried away.

Through this horrible confrontation everything in his

being was violently shaken. For a moment he was torn out of his grief, his ill humor, his indifferent passivity. He was overcome by an irresistible urge to intervene and seized by an inexpressible desire to save the man. He felt him to be so miserable, he found him even as a criminal so innocent, he identified with his situation so strongly, that he fully believed he could also convince others of it. He already wished to be able to speak for him, the most animated defense was already rising to his lips; he hastened to the hunting lodge and on the way could not refrain from speaking half aloud everything he wanted to lay before the steward.

When he entered the room he found Albert present, which put him out of sorts for a moment, but he composed himself and passionately presented his ideas to the steward, who shook his head a few times, and although Werther argued with the greatest animation, passion, and veracity that a person can employ to excuse someone, the steward, as one may easily imagine, was not swayed by it. On the contrary, he did not let our friend finish, energetically contradicted him, and blamed him for taking a murderer under his wing! He pointed out that in this fashion every law would be annulled, the security of the state would be destroyed, and furthermore, he added, in such a matter he could do nothing without taking the gravest responsibility upon himself. Everything would have to take its orderly, prescribed course.

Werther did not yet yield but only asked that the steward might look the other way if someone were to help the man to flee. The steward rejected this too. Albert, finally joining the conversation, took the old man's side. Werther was outvoted and, suffering horribly, set off, after the steward had told him several times: No, he is not to be saved!

How great an impression these words must have made on him we can see from a note that was found among his papers, and that was certainly written the same day:

"You are not to be saved, wretch! I clearly see that we are not to be saved."

Albert's last remarks about the case of the prisoner, spoken in the steward's presence, had been highly repugnant to Werther: he thought he saw in them some touchiness toward himself, and even though after considerable reflection it did not escape his astuteness that both men might be right, still it seemed to him he would have to deny his innermost being if he were to confess or concede it.

We find among his papers a note relating to this that perhaps expresses his entire relation to Albert.

"What good is it for me to tell myself again and again that he is upstanding and good, it tears me apart inside; I cannot be just."

Because it was a mild evening and the weather was just inclining to thaw, Lotte returned home with Albert on foot. Along the way she looked around here and there, as if she missed Werther's company. Albert began to talk about him; by being just to him he blamed him. He touched on Werther's unfortunate passion, and wished it were possible to have him leave.—I wish it also for our sakes, he said, and I beg you, he went on, see to it that you give his behavior toward you a different direction, and reduce his too frequent visits. People are noticing, and I know that there has been some talk about it.—Lotte was silent, and Albert seemed to feel her silence; at least after that time he no longer mentioned Werther to her, and if she mentioned him he dropped the conversation or directed it to other matters.

The vain attempt that Werther made to rescue the unfortunate man was the last blazing up of the flame of a dying light; he sank ever deeper into pain and inactivity; particularly, he was almost beside himself when he heard that he might even be summoned as a witness against the man, who was now denying his guilt.

Everything unpleasant in his public life, his vexation at the embassy, whatever else had turned out badly, whatever had hurt him, surged and ebbed in his soul. With all this, he found himself justified in his inactivity, cut off from all prospects, incapable of seizing any handle to get hold of the ordinary business of life, and so he finally descended, yielding completely to his strange feeling, his way of thinking, and submitting to his endless passion, to the everlasting monotony of being sad and mournful company for the charming and beloved creature whose peace he disturbed, his energies raging, venting them without aim or prospect, ever closer to a sad end.

Several letters he left behind, which we would like to insert here, bear the strongest witness to his confusion, his passion, his restless activity and strivings, and his weariness with life.

DECEMBER 12

Dear Wilhelm, I am in a state which those wretches must have been in of whom one believed that they were being tossed about by an evil spirit. Sometimes it overcomes me: it is not fear, not desire—it is some inner, unknown raging that threatens to tear open my breast, that stifles my throat! Woe! Woe! And then I wander around in the horrible nocturnal scenes of this inhuman season of the year.

Last evening I had to get outdoors. There had been a

sudden thaw; I had heard that the river was flooding, all the brooks were swollen, and my whole dear valley below Wahlheim was underwater! After eleven I ran out into the night. A horrendous spectacle, seeing the churning waters swirling down from the rock in the moonlight, over fields and meadows and hedges and everything, and up and down the broad valley a single raging lake whipped by the wind! And when the moon came out again and rested above the black clouds, and the flood stretching out before me rolled and resounded in the terrible, glorious reflection, I was overcome by a shudder and then by a longing! Oh, I stood above the abyss with outstretched arms and breathed: down! down! and lost myself in the bliss of flinging down my torments, my sufferings! To roar away like the waves! Oh!—but you were not able to lift your foot from the ground and end all your torments!—My clock has not yet run out, I feel it! O Wilhelm, how gladly would I have given my human existence to tear along like clouds with the winds of every storm, to embrace the floods! Ha! And will not one day perhaps this bliss be granted this imprisoned soul?—

And as I looked down wistfully on a small spot where I had rested with Lotte under a willow on a hot walk—that too was flooded, and I hardly recognized the willow, Wilhelm! And her meadows, I thought, and the area around her hunting lodge! Our arbor, now upset by the rending stream! I thought. And the past's ray of sunlight appeared the way a prisoner dreams of meadows, herds, and high offices! I stood there!—I am not blaming myself, for I have the courage to die.—I would have— Now I'm sitting here like an old woman who gleans her wood from fence posts and her bread at strange doors in order to prolong and relieve her fading, joyless existence for yet another moment.

DECEMBER 14

What is this, my friend? I am frightened at myself! Is not my love for her the holiest, purest, most fraternal love? Have I ever felt a criminal desire in my soul?—I don't want to protest my innocence. And now, dreams! Oh, how truly those people felt who ascribed such contradictory effects to alien powers! Last night! I tremble to say it, I held her in my arms, firmly pressed against my breast, and covered her mouth that was whispering love with unending kisses; my eyes were swimming in the intoxication of hers! God! Am I criminal that even now I feel blissful recalling so intensely these burning joys! Lotte! Lotte!—And I am finished! My mind is all confused, for a week I have had no power of consciousness, my eyes are filled with tears. I am happy nowhere and happy everywhere. I wish nothing, desire nothing. It would be better for me if I went away.

The resolve to leave the world had at this time, under such conditions, grown stronger and stronger in Werther's soul. Since he had come back to Lotte it had always been his ultimate prospect and hope; but, he had told himself, it should not be an overhasty, precipitous deed, but a step he wanted to take with the firmest conviction, with the greatest possible resolve.

His doubts, his struggles with himself, can be glimpsed in an undated note found among his papers that appears to be the beginning of a letter to Wilhelm.

Her presence, her destiny, her empathy for mine presses the last tears from my scorched brain.

To raise the curtain and step behind it! That is all! But why the hesitation and delay? Because one doesn't know what it looks like there? And one doesn't return? And that is now the characteristic of our mind, to project darkness and confusion where we know nothing definite.

Finally he became increasingly reconciled and easy with the sad thought, and his intention became firm and irrevocable, as witnessed by the following ambiguous letter that he wrote to his friend.

DECEMBER 20

I thank your love, Wilhelm, for having caught that word. Yes, you are right: it would be better for me to leave. I am not entirely pleased by your proposal to come back to you; at least I would gladly like to make a detour, especially since we have the prospect of a persisting frost and good roads. It is also very kind of you to want to come fetch me; please wait another two weeks and for a letter from me with further details. It is important that nothing be plucked before it is ripe. And two weeks more or less can accomplish much. Tell my mother to pray for her son, and that I beg her forgiveness for all the vexation I have caused her. It has been my fate to sadden her to whom I owed joy. Farewell, dearest friend! May all the blessings of heaven be upon you! Farewell!

What was going on in Lotte's soul during this time, what her thoughts were about her husband, about her unfortunate friend, we are hardly able to express in words, although from what we know of her character we can confidently arrive at a quiet estimation, imagine a beautiful feminine soul such as hers, and feel with her.

So much is certain, that she had firmly resolved to do everything to have Werther leave, and if she hesitated it was out of warm, friendly concern because she knew how much it would cost him, indeed that it would be almost impossible for him. But at this time she was under greater pressure to be serious: her husband was totally silent about the relationship, as she too had always been silent about it, and this gave her the more reason to prove to him by a deed how her attitudes were the same as his.

On the same day that Werther wrote the previously inserted letter to his friend, it was the Sunday before Christmas, he came to Lotte in the evening and found her alone. She was busy arranging some toys she had got ready to give her little brothers and sisters as Christmas presents. He spoke about the pleasure the little ones would have, and of the times an unexpected opening of the door and the sight of a tree decorated with wax candles, sugarplums, and apples would make them gloriously happy.—You will get presents too, Lotte said, hiding her embarrassment beneath a gentle smile, if you are really nice; a little candlestick, and other things.—And what do you mean by nice? he exclaimed, how should I be, how can I be? Dearest Lotte!—Thursday evening is Christmas Eve, she said, the children are coming, my father too, everyone will receive his present, you come too—but not before.—Werther was brought up short. I beg you, she went on, that's the way it is, I beg you for the sake of my peace, it can't go on this way, it can't.—He turned his eyes away from her and paced up and down the room, muttering, "It can't go on this way," between his teeth. Lotte, who felt the terrible state her words had put him in, tried to distract him with all sorts of questions, but in vain.—No, Lotte! he exclaimed: I shall not see you again!—Why not? she replied. Werther, you can, you must see us again, but control yourself. Oh, why did you have to be born with this fierceness, this uncontrollable passion that fastens on everything you touch! I beg you, she continued, taking him by the hand, control yourself! Your mind, your knowledge, your talents, how many delights they offer you! Be a man! Turn this sad devotion away from a creature who can do nothing but feel sorry for you.—He ground his teeth and looked at her gloomily. She held his hand: Werther! she said. Just one moment of quiet reflection. Don't you feel that you are deceiving yourself, deliberately destroying yourself? Why me, Werther, why precisely me, the property of another? Precisely that? I fear, I fear it is only the impossibility of possessing me that makes this wish so attractive to you. He pulled his hand away from hers, looking at her with a fixed, angry glance.—Wise! he called out. Very wise! Was it perhaps Albert who made that remark? Politic! Very politic!—Anyone could make it, she replied. And should there not be in the whole wide world a girl who could fulfill your heart's desire? Get hold of yourself, go look for her, and I swear to you, you shall find her; for I have long been disturbed, for you and for us, by the isolation you have shut yourself up in while you have been here. Get hold of yourself! A trip will distract you, must distract you! Seek, find, an object worthy of your love, and come back and let us enjoy the blessedness of a true friendship together!

You could print that, he said with a cold smile, and recommend it to every schoolmaster. Dear Lotte! Leave me yet a little peace, it will all change!—But, Werther, the one condition, that you do not come back before Christmas Eve!—He was about to respond when Albert entered the room. They bade each other a frosty good evening and paced up and down in embarrassment beside each other. Werther began a trivial discussion that soon petered out, Albert did the same, and then asked his wife about certain instructions, and when he heard that they had not yet been carried out directed some words to her that seemed to Werther cold, indeed hard. He wanted to leave, could not, and hesitated until eight o'clock, his annoyance and displeasure constantly increasing, until the table was set and he took his hat and stick. Albert invited him to stay, but he, who thought he was hearing only an insignificant politeness, thanked him coldly and went away.

He came home, took the candle from the hand of his boy, who wanted to light his way, and went alone to his room, wept aloud, spoke angrily with himself, paced agitatedly back and forth, and finally threw himself on the bed in his clothes, where the servant found him when he dared to enter the room around eleven, to ask whether his master would like him to take off his boots, which Werther allowed, and forbade the servant to come into the room the next morning before he was called.

Early Monday, December 21, he wrote the following letter to Lotte, which after his death was found sealed on his table and delivered to her, and which I want to insert here by paragraphs, the way it was written, judging from the circumstances.

It is decided, Lotte, I want to die, and I write you this without romantic exaggeration, calmly, on the morning of the day on which I shall see you for the last time. When you read this, my dearest, the cool grave will cover the stiff remains of the restless unfortunate, who knows no greater sweetness in the final moments of his life than to converse with you. I have had a horrible night, but oh! one that did me good. The night strengthened my resolve, determined it: I want to die! As I tore myself away from you yesterday, my senses in a fearful uproar, how it all rushed to my heart, and my hopeless, joyless existence at your side seized me with horrible coldness— I barely reached my room, I threw myself on my knees, beside myself, and, dear God, You granted me the ultimate relief of the bitterest tears! A thousand violent shocks, a thousand prospects raged through my soul, and finally it was there, firm, whole, this one final thought: I want to die!—I lay down, and in the morning, in the calm of waking, it is still firm, still quite strong in my heart: I want to die!—It is not despair, it is certainty that I have settled on, and that I am sacrificing myself for you. Yes, Lotte! Why should I keep silent? One of us three must go, and I want it to be me! O my dearest! It has often slunk around my torn, raging heart—to murder your husband!—you!—myself!—So be it then!—When you climb the mountain on a lovely summer evening, then remember me as I so often came up the valley, and then look over at the cemetery, at my grave, at how the wind blows the high grass back and forth in the glow of the setting sun.—I was calm when I began, now, now I am crying like a child, as all this becomes so vivid around me.—

Around ten Werther called his servant, and while dressing told him how in a few days he would be going on a trip, so he should brush his clothes and get them ready to pack; he also ordered him to settle all his accounts, retrieve several books he had lent, and arrange to have payments made two months in advance to some poor people to whom he was accustomed to give something every week.

He had his meal brought to his room and afterwards rode out to the steward, whom he did not find at home. He walked up and down the garden profoundly absorbed, and seemed finally to want to pile up all the melancholy of memory on himself.

The little ones did not leave him long in peace, they ran after him, jumped up on him, told him that when it was tomorrow and tomorrow again and still one more day they would get their Christmas presents at Lotte's, and told him miracles corresponding to their small powers of imagination.—Tomorrow! he exclaimed. And tomorrow again! And still one more day!—And kissed them all warmly and was about to leave when the littlest boy wanted to whisper something in his ear. He revealed to him that his big brothers had already written beautiful New Year's wishes, so big! One for Papa, one for Lotte and Albert, and one for Herr Werther too; they wanted to present them early on New Year's Day. That overwhelmed him: he gave something to each, mounted his horse, left greetings for the old man, and rode away with tears in his eyes.

He came home around five, ordered the maid to see to the fire and keep it going into the night. He bade the servant pack books and linen in the bottom of the trunk and carefully fold up the clothes. After this he apparently wrote the following paragraph of his final letter to Lotte.

You do not expect me! You think I would obey and see you again only on Christmas Eve! To see you again, Lotte! Today or never again. Christmas Eve you will be holding this paper in your hand, trembling and wetting it with your sweet tears. I want to, I must! Oh, how happy I am to have made up my mind.

Lotte meanwhile had fallen into a strange state. After her last conversation with Werther she had felt how hard it would be for her to separate from him, and what he would suffer if he were to leave her.

It had been said in Albert's presence, as if in passing, that Werther would not come back before Christmas, and Albert had ridden off to see an official in the neighborhood with whom he had some business and where he was to remain overnight.

She was now sitting alone; none of her brothers and sisters were around her. She abandoned herself to her thoughts, silently mulling over her relationships. She saw herself eternally bound to the man whose love and devotion she knew, to whom she was wholeheartedly devoted, whose calm, whose dependability seemed to have been destined by heaven for a good woman to base the happiness of her life upon; she felt what he would always be to her and her children. On the other hand, Werther had become so dear to her; from the first moment of their friendship, the accord of their natures had revealed itself so wonderfully, her long acquaintance with him and so many situations they had been through together had made an indelible impression on her heart. She was accustomed to share with him everything interesting that she felt and thought, and his departure threatened to tear in her entire being a hole that could not be filled again. Oh, if she could have transformed him at that moment into a brother, how happy she would have been!—If she had been able to marry him off to one of her friends, if she could have hoped to re-pair his relationship with Albert!

She had thought about her friends one after another, but found with each one something to object to, found none she was willing to give him to.

Underneath all these observations she felt deeply, with-out making it clear to herself, that her secret heart's desire was to keep him for herself, but she said to herself that she could not, must not keep him; her pure, beautiful nature, otherwise so easily able to help her through, felt the pres-sure of a melancholy whose prospect for happiness was barred. Her heart was oppressed, and a dark cloud lay over her eyes.

It was six-thirty when she heard Werther coming up the stairs and quickly recognized his step, his voice asking for her. How her heart beat at his arrival, we might almost say for the first time. She would gladly have had the servants tell him that she was not there, and when he came in she exclaimed in a kind of passionate confusion: You have not kept your word.—I promised nothing, was his answer.—You should at least have acceded to my wishes, she replied, I asked you for the peace of us both.

She was not entirely aware of what she was saying and just as little of what she was doing when she sent for some friends in order not to be alone with Werther. He put down a few books he had brought, asked after other people, and she wished that her friends would come soon, then that they would stay away. The maid came back with the news that both begged to be excused.

She wanted to have the maid sit in the adjoining room with her work, then she changed her mind. Werther was pacing up and down the room. She went over to the clavier and began a minuet, but it wouldn't come. She composed herself and calmly sat down by Werther, who had taken his usual place on the sofa.

Have you nothing to read? she said.—He had nothing.—Over there in the drawer, she began, is your translation of some of Ossian's songs; I haven't read them yet, for I always hoped to hear them from you, but we never had, never found the occasion.—He smiled, fetched the songs, a shudder came over him as he took them in his hands, and his eyes filled with tears as he glanced into them. He sat down and read:*

"Star of descending night! Fair is thy light in the west! thou that liftest thy unshorn head from thy cloud: thy steps are stately on thy hill. What dost thou behold in the plain? The stormy winds are laid. The murmur of the torrent comes from afar. Roaring waves climb the distant rock. The flies of evening are on their feeble wings: the hum of their course is in the field. What dost thou behold, fair light? But thou dost smile and depart. The waves come with joy around thee: they bathe thy lovely hair. Farewell, thou silent beam! Let the light of Ossian's soul arise!

And it does arise in its strength! I behold my departed friends. Their gathering is on Lora, as in the days of other years. Fingal comes like a watery column of mist! his heroes are around: and see the bards of song, gray-haired Ullin! Stately Ryno! Alpin with the tuneful voice! the soft complaint of Minona! How are ye changed, my friends, since the days of Selma's feast! when we contended, like

---

*"The Songs of Ossian" was a hoax perpetrated in the 1760s by James Macpherson, who claimed to have found ancient Gaelic writings. They became very popular, although their authenticity was soon questioned. The passages are here quoted from the English original, the "Songs of Selma." Goethe's translation makes Ossian sound more fluidly passionate than the original.—trans.

gales of spring, as they fly along the hill, and bend by turns the feebly whistling grass.

Minona came forth in her beauty: with downcast look and tearful eye. Her hair flew slowly on the blast that rushed unfrequent from the hill. The souls of the heroes were sad when she raised the tuneful voice. Often had they seen the grave of Salgar, the dark dwelling of white-bosomed Colma. Colma left alone on the hill, with all her voice of song! Salgar promised to come: but the night descended around. Hear the voice of Colma, when she sat alone on the hill.

Colma: It is night, I am alone, forlorn on the hill of storms. The wind is heard on the mountain. The torrent pours down the rock. No hut receives me from the rain; forlorn on the hill of winds!

Rise, moon! from behind thy clouds. Stars of the night, arise! Lead me, some light, to the place where my love rests from the chase alone! his bow near him, unstrung: his dogs panting around him. But here I must sit alone, by the rock of the mossy stream. The stream and the wind roar aloud. I hear not the voice of my love! Why delays my Salgar, why the chief of the hill, his promise? here is the rock, and here the tree! here is the roaring stream! Thou didst promise with night to be here. Ah! whither is my Salgar gone? With thee, I would fly from my father; with thee, from my brother of pride. Our race have long been foes; we are not foes, O Salgar!

Cease a little while, O wind! stream, be thou silent awhile! let my voice be heard around. Let my wanderer hear me! Salgar! it is Colma who calls. Here is the tree, and the rock. Salgar, my love! I am here. Why delayest thou thy coming? Lo! the calm moon comes forth. The flood is bright in the vale. The rocks are gray on the steep, I see him not on the brow. His dogs come not before him, with tidings of his near approach. Here I must sit alone!

Who lie on the heath beside me? Are they my love and my brother? Speak to me, O my friends! To Colma they give no reply. Speak to me; I am alone! My soul is tormented with fears! Ah! they are dead! Their swords are red from the fight. O my brother! my brother! why hast thou slain my Salgar? why, O Salgar! hast thou slain my brother? Dear were ye both to me! what shall I say in your praise? Thou wert fair on the hill among thousands! he was terrible in fight. Speak to me; hear my voice; hear me, song of my love! They are silent; silent for ever! Cold, cold, are their breasts of clay! Oh! from the rock on the hill, from the top of the windy steep, speak, ye ghosts of the dead! speak, I will not be afraid! Whither are ye gone to rest? In what cave of the hill shall I find the departed? No feeble voice is on the gale, no answer half-drowned in the storm!

I sit in my grief; I wait for morning in my tears! Rear the tomb, ye friends of the dead. Close it not till Colma come. My life flies away like a dream: why should I stay behind? Here shall I rest with my friends, by the stream of the sounding rock. When night comes on the hill; when the loud winds arise; my ghost shall stand in the blast, and mourn the death of my friends. The hunter shall hear from his booth, he shall fear but love my voice! For sweet shall my voice be for my friends: pleasant were her friends to Colma!

Such was thy song, Minona, softly blushing daughter of Torman. Our tears descended for Colma, and our souls were sad! Ullin came with his harp! he gave the song of Alpin. The voice of Alpin was pleasant: the soul of Ryno was a beam of fire! But they had rested in the narrow house: their voice had ceased in Selma. Ullin had returned, one day, from the chase, before the heroes fell. He heard their strife on the hill; their song was soft but sad! They mourned the fall of Morar, first of mortal men! His soul was like the soul of Fingal: his sword like the sword of Oscar. But he fell, and his father mourned: his sister's eyes were full of tears. Minona's eyes were full of tears, the sister of car-borne Morar. She retired from the song of Ullin, like the moon in the west, when she foresees the shower and hides her fair head in a cloud. I touched the harp with Ullin; the song of mourning rose!

Ryno: The wind and the rain are past; calm is the noon of day. The clouds are divided in heaven. Over the green hills flies the inconstant sun. Red through the stony vale comes down the stream of the hill. Sweet are thy murmurs, O stream! but more sweet is the voice I hear. It is the voice of Alpin, the son of song, mourning for the dead! Bent is his head of age; red his tearful eye. Alpin, thou son of song, why alone on the silent hill? why complainest thou, as a blast in the wood; as a wave on the lonely shore?

Alpin: My tears, O Ryno! are for the dead; my voice for those that have passed away. Tall thou art on the hill; fair among the sons of the vale. But thou shalt fall like Morar; the mourner shall sit on thy tomb. The hills shall know thee no more; thy bow shall be in thy hall unstrung.

Thou wert swift, O Morar! as a roe on the desert; terrible as a meteor of fire. Thy wrath was as the storm. Thy sword in battle, as lightning in the field. Thy voice was a stream after rain; like thunder on distant hills. Many fell by thy arm; they were consumed in the flames of thy wrath. But when thou didst return from war, how peaceful was thy brow! Thy face was like the sun after rain; like the moon in the silence of night; calm as the breast of the lake when the loud wind is laid.

Narrow is thy dwelling now! Dark the place of thine abode! With three steps I compass thy grave. O thou who wast so great before! Four stones, with their heads of moss, are the only memorial of thee. A tree with scarce a leaf, long grass, which whistles in the wind, mark to the hunter's eye the grave of the mighty Morar. Morar! thou art low indeed. Thou hast no mother to mourn thee; no maid with her tears of love. Dead is she that brought thee forth. Fallen is the daughter of Morglan.

Who on his staff is this? who is this whose head is white with age; whose eyes are red with tears? who quakes at every step? It is thy father, O Morar! the father of no son but thee. He heard of thy fame in war; he heard of foes dispersed. He heard of Morar's renown; why did he not hear of his wound? Weep, thou father of Morar! weep; but thy son heareth thee not. Deep is the sleep of the dead; low their pillow of dust. No more shall he hear thy voice; no more awake at thy call. When shall it be morn in the grave, to bid the slumberer awake? Farewell, thou bravest of men! thou conqueror in the field! but the field shall see thee no more; nor the dark wood be lightened with the splendor of thy steel. Thou hast left no son. The song shall preserve thy name. Future times shall hear of thee; they shall hear of the fallen Morar.

The grief of all arose, but most the bursting sigh of Armin. He remembers the death of his son, who fell in the days of his youth. Carmor was near the hero, the chief of the echoing Galmal. Why burst the sigh of Armin? he said. Is there a cause to mourn? The song comes, with its music, to melt and please the soul. It is like soft mist, that, rising from a lake, pours on the silent vale; the green flowers are filled with dew, but the sun returns in his strength, and the mist is gone. Why art thou sad, O Armin, chief of sea-surrounded Gorma?

Sad I am! nor small is my cause of woe. Carmor, thou hast lost no son; thou hast lost no daughter of beauty. Colgar the valiant lives; and Annira, fairest maid. The boughs of thy house ascend, O Carmor! but Armin is the last of his race. Dark is thy bed, O Daura! deep thy sleep in the tomb! When shalt thou awake with thy songs? with all thy voice of music?

Arise, winds of autumn, arise; blow along the heath! streams of the mountains, roar! roar, tempests, in the groves of my oaks! walk through broken clouds, O moon! show thy pale face, at intervals! bring to my mind the night, when all my children fell; when Arindal the mighty fell! when Daura the lovely failed! Daura, my daughter! thou wert fair; fair as the moon on Fura, white as the driven snow; sweet as the breathing gale. Arindal, thy bow was strong. Thy spear was swift on the field. Thy look was like mist on the wave: thy shield, a red cloud in a storm. Armar, renowned in war, came, and sought Daura's love. He was not long refused: fair was the hope of their friends!

Erath, son of Odgal, repined: his brother had been slain by Armar. He came disguised like a son of the sea: fair was his skiff on the wave; white his locks of age; calm his serious brow. Fairest of women, he said, lovely daughter of Armin! a rock not distant in the sea bears a tree on its side: red shines the fruit afar! There Armar waits for Daura. I come to carry his love! She went; she called on Armar. Nought answered, but the son of the rock. Armar, my love! my love! why tormentest thou me with fear! hear, son of Arnart, hear: it is Daura who calleth thee! Erath the traitor fled laughing to the land. She lifted up her voice; she called for her brother and for her father. Arindal! Armin! none to relieve your Daura!

Her voice came over the sea. Arindal my son descended from the hill; rough in the spoils of the chase. His arrows rattled by his side; his bow was in his hand; five dark gray dogs attended his steps. He saw fierce Erath on the shore: he seized and bound him to an oak. Thick wind the thongs of the hide around his limbs: he loads the winds with his groans. Arindal ascends the deep in his boat, to bring Daura to land. Armar came in his wrath, and let fly the gray-feathered shaft. It sunk, it sunk in thy heart, O Arindal, my son! for Erath the traitor thou diest. The oar is stopped at once; he panted on the rock and expired. What is thy grief, O Daura, when round thy feet is poured thy brother's blood! The boat is broke in twain. Armar plunges into the sea, to rescue his Daura, or die. Sudden a blast from a hill came over the waves. He sunk, and he rose no more.

Alone on the sea-beat rock, my daughter was heard to complain. Frequent and loud were her cries. What could her father do? All night I stood on the shore. I saw her by the faint beam of the moon. All night I heard her cries. Loud was the wind; the rain beat hard on the hill. Before morning appeared her voice was weak, it died away, like the evening breeze among the grass of the rocks. Spent with grief, she expired; and left thee, Armin, alone. Gone is my strength in war! fallen my pride among women! When the storms aloft arise; when the north lifts the wave on high! I sit by the sounding shore, and look on the fatal rock. Often by the setting moon, I see the ghosts of my children. Half viewless, they walk in mournful conference together."

A stream of tears that poured from Lotte's eyes and relieved her oppressed heart interrupted Werther's recitation. He threw down the papers, seized her hand, and wept the bitterest tears. Lotte leaned on her other hand and hid her eyes with her handkerchief. Both were in a dreadful state. They felt their own misery in the fate of the noble heroes, felt it jointly, and their tears united them. Werther's lips and eyes burned on Lotte's arms; a shudder came over her; she wanted to draw back, but pain and sympathy lay on her as numbing as lead. She breathed to recover herself, and sobbing, begged him to go on, begged him with the whole voice of heaven! Werther trembled, his heart was about to burst, he picked up the page and read half brokenly:

"Why dost thou awake me, O gale? It seems to say: I am covered with the drops of heaven. The time of my fading is near, the blast that shall scatter my leaves. Tomorrow shall the traveler come; he that saw me in my beauty shall come. His eyes will search the field, but they will not find me."*

The whole weight of these words fell on the unfortunate man. Frantic with despair, he threw himself down before Lotte, seized her hands, pressed them to his eyes, against his forehead, and an intimation of his terrible purpose seemed to fly through her soul. Her senses became confused, she pressed his hands, pressed them against her breast, bent down to him with a melancholy gesture, and their burning cheeks touched. The world was blotted out for them. He threw his arms around her, pressed her to his breast, and covered her trembling, stammering lips with raging kisses.—Werther! she called out in a suffocated voice, turning away, Werther!—and with a weak hand pushed his breast from hers.—Werther! she cried in the composed tone of the noblest feeling.—He did not resist, released

*Goethe translated this paragraph from another of Ossian's poems, "Berrathon."—trans.

her from his arms, and threw himself down senseless before her. She tore herself away, and in fearful confusion, trembling between love and anger, she said: This is the last time! Werther! You shall not see me again.—And with a glance full of love at the poor unfortunate, she hastened into the adjoining room, locking the door behind her. Werther stretched out his arms after her, did not dare hold her back. He lay on the floor, his head on the sofa, and remained in this position for more than half an hour, until a noise brought him to his senses. It was the maid, who wanted to set the table. He paced up and down the room, and when he found himself alone again went to the door of the adjoining room and called out in a soft voice: Lotte! Lotte! Just one more word! A farewell!—She was silent. He waited and begged and waited; then he tore himself away and cried: Farewell, Lotte! Farewell forever!

He came to the town gate. The watchmen, who were used to him, silently let him out. It was blowing between rain and snow, and it was only toward eleven that he knocked to be let back in. When Werther arrived home, his servant noticed that he had lost his hat. He did not dare say anything, helped him undress, everything was wet. Afterwards, his hat was found on a rock that overlooks the valley from the side of a hill, and it is incomprehensible how he had climbed there on a dark, wet night without plummeting down.

He went to bed and slept long. When the servant was called the next morning to bring coffee, he found Werther writing. He wrote the following in his letter to Lotte.

———

For the last time, then, for the last time I open these eyes. Alas! They will never again see the sun, a gloomy, misty day keeps it hid. So then, Nature, grieve! Your son, your friend, your beloved, nears his end. Lotte, it is a feeling unlike any other, and yet it comes closest to a glimmering dream to say to oneself: This is the last morning. The last! Lotte, I have no feeling for the expression "the last"! Am I not standing here in all my strength, and tomorrow I shall lie stretched out limp on the ground. To die! What does it mean? Look, we dream when we talk about death. I have seen many people die; but so limited is mankind that it has no sense of the beginning and end of its existence. Existence that is now still mine, yours! Yours, O beloved! And a moment—separated, parted—perhaps forever? No, Lotte, no.—How can I perish? How can you perish? We *are*!—Perish!—What does that mean? It's just another word! An empty sound, without stirring feeling in my heart.—Dead, Lotte! Hurriedly thrown into the cold earth, so narrow! so dark!—I had a friend who was everything to me in my helpless youth; she died, and I followed her corpse and stood at the grave when they lowered the coffin and pulled the ropes out from under it with a scraping sound and brought them up, then the first shovelsful rained down clumps of earth and the fearful box gave off a muffled sound, more and more muffled, and was finally covered!—I threw myself down beside the grave—overcome, shaken, afraid, torn apart inside; but I did not know what was happening to me—what will happen to me.—To die! Grave! I don't understand the word!

Oh, forgive me! Forgive me! Yesterday! It should have been the final moment of my life. O you angel! For the first time, for the first time the feeling of bliss glowed freed from doubt through my innermost being: She loves me! She loves me! Still burning on my lips is the divine fire that streamed from yours; there is a new warm bliss in my heart. Forgive me! Forgive me!

Oh, I knew you loved me, knew it from the first soulful glances, from the first pressure of your hand, and yet when I left you, when I saw Albert at your side, I lost heart again in feverish doubts.

Do you remember the flowers you sent me when at that fateful ball you could not address a word to me, not reach out your hand to me? Oh, I knelt before them for half the night, and they were the seal of your love for me. But alas! these impressions passed, the way the feeling of the grace of the believer's God, granted him in visible sacred signs with all the fullness of heaven, gradually fades again from his soul.

All that is transitory, but no eternity will extinguish the glowing life I feel within me that I enjoyed yesterday on your lips! She loves me! This arm has embraced her, these lips have trembled on hers, this mouth has stammered on hers: she is mine! You are mine! Yes, Lotte, forever.

And what does it signify that Albert is your husband? Husband! That would be for this world—and for this world it is sin that I love you, that I would like to tear you from his arms to mine. Sin? Good! And I am punishing myself for it; I have tasted it in all its heavenly bliss, this sin, have sucked strength and life's balm into my heart. From this moment you are mine! Mine, dear Lotte! I am going on ahead, to my Father, to your Father. To Him will I pour out my misfortune, and He will comfort me until you come, and I will fly to you and embrace you and remain with you in eternal embrace before the countenance of the infinite.

I am not dreaming, not imagining! Close to the grave, things are becoming clearer to me. We will be! We shall see each other again! See your mother! I will see her, will find her, and oh, empty my whole heart out before her! Your mother, your image.

———

Toward eleven Werther asked his servant whether Albert had returned. The servant said yes, he had seen his horse being led there. At this Werther gave him an open note, saying:

"Would you be so kind as to lend me your pistols for a trip I am undertaking? Farewell!"

Lotte had slept little the past night; what she had feared was decided, decided in a way that she could neither foresee nor fear. Her blood that formerly flowed easy and pure was in feverish turmoil, a thousand different feelings shook her lovely heart. Was it the fire of Werther's embraces that she felt in her breast? Was it indignation at his audacity? Was it an unpleasant comparison of her present state with those days of free, uninhibited innocence and carefree confidence in herself? How was she to face her husband? How confess to him a scene that she could confess in good conscience, yet did not trust herself to confess? They had for so long been silent with each other, and should she be the first to break this silence and, at just the wrong time, reveal to him such an unexpected discovery? She already feared that just hearing of Werther's visit would make an unpleasant impression on him, and now this unexpected catastrophe! Could she hope that her husband would see it in the proper light, entirely without prejudice? And could she wish that he might read her soul? And still again, could she dissimulate toward a man before whom she had always been open and free, like a clear crystal glass, and from whom she had never kept nor could keep a single one of her feelings? All these things worried her and made her embarrassed; and her thoughts kept constantly returning to Werther, who was lost to her, whom she could not let go of, whom she must, alas! leave to his own devices and to whom, if he had lost her, nothing else remained.

She could not at this moment clearly realize how heavily the impasse between herself and Albert weighed upon her. Such good, such reasonable people began on account of certain concealed differences to be mute with one another, each reflected on his being right and the other wrong, and their relations became tangled and inflamed to such a degree that it was impossible to cut the knot at this critical moment on which everything depended. If a happy trust had brought them closer to each other again sooner, if mutual love and consideration had sprung up between them and opened their hearts, perhaps our friend might still have been saved.

Another strange circumstance was involved. As we know from his letters, Werther had never made a secret of his longing to quit this world. Albert had often argued with him about it, and Lotte and her husband had sometimes spoken of it. Albert, who felt a strong repugnance about the act, had often maintained with a sort of feeling otherwise alien to his character that he found reason to very much doubt the seriousness of such an intention; he had even permitted himself to joke about it, and imparted his skepticism to Lotte. On the one hand this calmed her when her thoughts brought the sad image to her mind, but on the other she felt it prevented her from sharing with her husband the worries that were tormenting her at this moment.

Albert returned, and Lotte went to meet him with embarrassed haste. He was not cheerful, his business had not been concluded, he had found the neighboring steward to be an inflexible, small-minded man. The bad roads had also made him irritable.

He asked whether anything had happened, and she answered overhastily that Werther had been there the evening before. He asked whether letters had arrived, and received the response that a letter and some parcels lay in his room. He went there, and Lotte remained alone. The presence of the man she honored and loved made a new impression on her heart. The memory of his magnanimity, his love and goodness, had further calmed her being, she felt secretly drawn to follow him, she took up her work and went to his room, as she was often accustomed to do. She found him busy opening and reading the parcels. Several seemed not to contain the most pleasant information. She put a few questions to him that he answered curtly, and he went to his desk to write.

They had been sitting beside each other in this manner for an hour, and it was getting gloomier and gloomier in Lotte's mind. She felt how hard it would be for her to reveal to her husband, even if he was in the best of spirits, what lay on her heart; she fell into a melancholy that made her the more anxious as she tried to hide it, and she sought to choke back her tears.

The appearance of Werther's servant caused her the greatest embarrassment. He handed the note to Albert, who turned calmly to his wife and said: Give him the pistols.— I wish him a pleasant journey, he said to the boy.—That struck like a lightning bolt, she tottered to her feet, she did not know what was happening to her. Slowly she went over to the wall, trembling took down the pistols, wiped them off, hesitated, and would have delayed still longer if Albert had not compelled her by a questioning look. She handed the unhappy instruments to the boy without being able to utter a word, and when he was out of the house she picked up her work and went to her room in a state of the most inexpressible uncertainty. Her heart prophesied all sorts of horrors. Soon she was on the point of casting herself at her husband's feet, revealing everything to him, the story of the previous evening, her guilt and her presentiments. Then again she saw no way out of such an undertaking, least of all could she hope to talk her husband into going to Werther. The table was set, and a good friend who had come to ask something, intending to leave again directly, stayed, making the conversation at the meal bearable; one forced oneself, one spoke, one talked, one forgot oneself.

The boy came to Werther with the pistols, he took them with delight when he heard that Lotte had handed them to him. He had bread and wine brought, told the boy to go eat, and sat down to write.

They have passed through your hands, you have wiped the dust from them, I kiss them a thousand times, you have touched them: and you, spirit of heaven, favor my resolve! And you, Lotte, hand me the instrument, you from whose hands I wished to receive death and now receive it. Oh, I interrogated my boy, you trembled as you handed them to him, you said no farewell!—Woe! Woe! No farewell!— Could you have closed your heart to me for the sake of the moment that eternally bound me to you? Lotte, no millenium can erase the impression! And, I feel it, you cannot hate him who burns for you so.

After eating he bade the boy pack up everything, tore up many papers, went out and settled a few remaining debts. He came home again, went out again outside the town gate, ignoring the rain, into the Count's garden, wandered around some more in the area, returned as night was falling, and wrote:

Wilhelm, I have seen field and forest and sky for the last time. Farewell to you also! Dear Mother, pardon me! Comfort her, Wilhelm! God bless you both! My affairs are entirely in order. Farewell! We will see each other again, and happier.

Albert, I have repaid you badly, and you will forgive me. I have disturbed the peace of your house, I have brought mistrust between you. Farewell! I want to end it. Oh, that my death might make you both happy! Albert! Albert! Make the angel happy! And thus may God's blessing dwell over you!

He rummaged about a good deal in his papers throughout the evening, tore up many and threw them in the stove, sealed several parcels addressed to Wilhelm. They contained small essays, scattered thoughts, of which I have seen a number; and after he had a fire laid at ten o'clock and had a bottle of wine brought, he sent his servant, whose bedroom, like those of the other people of the household, was far out in back, to bed. The servant lay down in his clothes to be on hand early, for his master had said that the post horses would be in front of the house before six.

All is so quiet around me, and so calm my soul. I thank You, God, for giving me this warmth, this energy in these final moments.

I step to the window, my dearest! and see and still see through the rushing clouds flying by scattered stars of the eternal heavens! Stars, you will not fall! The Eternal One bears you on His heart, and me. I see the stars of the handle of the Big Dipper, the dearest of all constellations. When I left you at night, as I stepped out of your door, it was standing up there opposite me. With what intoxication did I often gaze at it! with upstretched hands make it the sign, the sacred token of my present happiness! And yet—O Lotte, what does not remind me of you! Where do you not surround me! And didn't I, like a dissatisfied child, grab to myself all sorts of trifles that you, divine one, had touched!

Dear silhouette! I bequeath it back to you, Lotte, and beg you to honor it. I have pressed thousands and thousands of kisses on it, waved to it a thousand greetings when I went out or came home.

In a note I have asked your father to take care of my body. In the churchyard, back in the corner toward the field, there are two linden trees; there I wish to rest. He can, he will, do that for his friend. You ask him too. I do not expect pious Christians to lay their bodies beside a poor unfortunate. Oh, I would like you to bury me by a road or in a lonely valley where priests and Levites would pass by and bless the identifying stone, and where the Samaritan would shed a tear.

Here, Lotte! I do not tremble to grasp the dreadful, cold

goblet from which I am to drink the giddiness of death! You handed it to me and I do not hesitate. All! All! Thus are all the desires and hopes of my life fulfilled! To knock so cold, so stiff, at the iron gates of death.

That I could have been blessed with the happiness of dying for you! Lotte, to give myself for you! I would die with courage, joyfully, if I could give you back the calm, the bliss of your life. But alas! It was only given to a few noble souls to spill their blood for their dear ones and through their death inspire a new, hundredfold life for their friends.

I wish to be buried, Lotte, in these clothes, you have touched them, consecrated them; I have asked this of your father, too. My soul hovers over the coffin. My pockets are not to be gone through. This pale red ribbon that you were wearing on your breast when I first found you, surrounded by your children—Oh, kiss them a thousand times and tell them the fate of their unfortunate friend! The dear ones! They swarm around me. Oh, how I fastened myself on you! From the first moment could not let you go!—This ribbon is to be buried with me. You gave it to me on my birthday! How I devoured it all!—Oh, I did not think that my path would lead to this!—Be still! I beg you, be still!—

They are loaded—it is striking twelve. So be it!—Lotte! Lotte! Farewell! Farewell!

A neighbor saw the flash of the powder and heard the shot; but since everything remained still he gave it no further notice.

At six in the morning the servant comes in with the lamp. He finds his master on the floor, the pistol, and blood. He calls out, he grasps him; no answer, only a rattle. He runs for the doctors, for Albert. Lotte hears the bell, a trembling seizes all her limbs. She wakes her husband, they get up, the servant, howling and stammering, brings them the news, Lotte sinks fainting before Albert.

When the doctor came to the unfortunate man he found him on the floor, beyond help, his pulse still beating, all his limbs paralyzed. He had shot himself in the head above the right eye, the brain was protruding. Pointlessly, a vein was opened in his arm, the blood flowed, he was still gasping for breath.

From the blood on the arm of the chair it could be deduced that he had committed the deed sitting at his table, that he had sunk down and convulsively twisted around the chair. He lay toward the window, inert, on his back, booted and completely clothed, in the blue coat and yellow vest.

The house, the neighborhood, the town were in an uproar. Albert came in. Werther had been laid on the bed, his forehead bound up, not moving a limb, his face already that of a dead man. His lungs were still rattling horribly, now weakly, now more strongly; his end was awaited.

He had drunk only a glass of the wine. *Emilia Galotti** lay open on the table.

Let me say nothing of Albert's consternation, of Lotte's misery.

The old steward came bursting in at the news, he kissed the dying man with the warmest tears. His oldest sons soon came after him on foot, they collapsed beside the bed, giving vent to the most unrestrained grief, kissed Werther's hands and mouth, and the oldest, whom he had always loved the most, hung on his lips until he died and the boy

---

*A play (1772) by G. E. Lessing.—trans.

was forcibly torn away. Werther died around noon. The presence of the steward and his preparations forestalled a commotion. Toward eleven at night he had Werther buried in the place he had chosen for himself. The old man followed the coffin and his sons, Albert was not able to. Lotte's life was feared for. Artisans carried him. No clergyman attended.

READING GROUP GUIDE

1. The idea of "family" is central to this novel. Make a list of all the families—whole, partial, substitutive, and metaphorical—that are found in *Young Werther*. What conclusions can you draw from this list?

2. Does Charlotte love Werther? Why can't she give him up?

3. The novel is filled with references to other literature: novels of ordinary life; the poet of feeling, Friedrich Klopstock; Homer; and Ossian. What relation do these have to the characters?

4. How does nature function in the novel to reflect the characters and action?

5. This is a novel in letters, but we only have Werther's letters (plus an editor at certain points). How does the reader know what the other characters, and the recipients of the letters, are feeling or thinking?

6. There are many references to religion in the book, Christian, pagan, and the religion of nature. How do they express themselves in the novel?

7. Werther's impulsive feelings are constantly colliding with everyday reality. Why is this so insistent in the novel, and why is his suicide so realistically presented?

8. Why does this novel, which was written in 1774 and revised by Goethe in 1787, seem so fresh and immediate today?

9. What does Werther bring into the lives of the other characters that they would be otherwise missing in their society?

ABOUT THE TRANSLATOR

BURTON PIKE is professor emeritus of comparative literature and German at the Graduate School of the City University of New York. He edited and co-translated Robert Musil's *The Man Without Qualities* and a book of Musil's essays, and his translations of prose and poetry from German and French have appeared in *Fiction, Grand Street, Conjunctions, Chicago Review,* and other magazines. He has had a Guggenheim Fellowship, and is a member of the PEN Translation Committee.

A NOTE ON THE TYPE

The principal text of this Modern Library edition
was set in a digitized version of Janson, a typeface that
dates from about 1690 and was cut by Nicholas Kis,
a Hungarian working in Amsterdam. The original matrices have
survived and are held by the Stempel foundry in Germany.
Hermann Zapf redesigned some of the weights and sizes for
Stempel, basing his revisions on the original design.

MODERN LIBRARY IS ONLINE AT
WWW.MODERNLIBRARY.COM

MODERN LIBRARY ONLINE IS YOUR GUIDE
TO CLASSIC LITERATURE ON THE WEB

THE MODERN LIBRARY E-NEWSLETTER

Our free e-mail newsletter is sent to subscribers, and features sample chapters, interviews with and essays by our authors, upcoming books, special promotions, announcements, and news.

To subscribe to the Modern Library e-newsletter, send a blank e-mail to: **sub_modernlibrary@info.randomhouse.com** or visit **www.modernlibrary.com**

THE MODERN LIBRARY WEBSITE

Check out the Modern Library website at
www.modernlibrary.com for:

- The Modern Library e-newsletter
- A list of our current and upcoming titles and series
- Reading Group Guides and exclusive author spotlights
- Special features with information on the classics and other paperback series
- Excerpts from new releases and other titles
- A list of our e-books and information on where to buy them
- The Modern Library Editorial Board's 100 Best Novels and 100 Best Nonfiction Books of the Twentieth Century written in the English language
- News and announcements

Questions? E-mail us at **modernlibrary@randomhouse.com**
For questions about examination or desk copies, please visit
the Random House Academic Resources site at
www.randomhouse.com/academic